Jai

Devil's Advocates, Volume 3

S L Davies

Published by S L Davies, 2022.

This is a work of fiction. Similarities to real people, places, or events are entirely coincidental.

JAI

First edition. September 13, 2022.

Copyright © 2022 S L Davies.

ISBN: 979-8215616949

Written by S L Davies.

D ylan
(17 years old)

"Dylan, I need you to come and sit down, I've got something I have to talk to you about," Papa said. The skin on his face was greying and his eyes held bags underneath. He hadn't been looking well lately and I'd been pushing for him to go and see the doctors.

"What is it, Papa?" I asked as I took a seat at the kitchen table in our tiny apartment. Since my Mama ran off when I was a kid, Papa did his best to keep a roof over our heads, but there wasn't much left once the bills were paid.

"I went to the doctors," Papa started with a sigh.

I frowned. This could only mean bad news, there was no way that he would pull me aside to talk to me if he had all the clear.

"I've been diagnosed with cancer. They found leukemia in my system."

I opened and closed my mouth as I stared at my Papa. The word cancer screamed at me. People died of cancer. There were medicines to help, but people every day, human and supernatural died of cancer.

"What does that mean Papa. I mean, I know what it means, but can't they fix you?" I asked.

"They are going to try. I've got to go to the hospital tomorrow for my first round of chemo. Dr. Rankin believes I've had it for a long time, but because of the supernatural healing it has kept it at bay, but it's bad son. I don't know if I'm going to make it through this one."

Papa's words were like a knife to my chest. He was the only one I had left. We'd never known what happened to Mama after she left. I came home from school one day and found the note she'd taped to the door saying she'd met someone and was leaving. I'd been so angry that I didn't give a shit if she lived or died. I had Papa. But now. Now I wasn't sure for how long.

"The only problem is that the chemo is expensive. I'm going to have to stop working, the chemo is going to hit my body hard."

"I'll get a job. It will be alright," I said with a shake of my head. There wasn't anything I wouldn't do to make sure my Papa lived.

Papa shook his head. "No, son, I want you to stay at school. Make something of yourself."

"There is time for that Papa. But there isn't time to make you well. I will leave school and get a job," I said firmly with my mind made up. "I'm not going to let you die."

Papa smiled and breathed out a long breath. "I'm going to have to die sometime son."

"You're still a young man Papa, you have a long time left."

Papa chuckled. "Last week you said I was old and needed to go to the doctors."

"Last week, I was an idiot."

Papa reached out his hand and took mine, giving it a squeeze. "I'll be here for as long as the creator sees fit. But when it is my time to go home, then I will gladly go. I won't try to stop fate. I've had a good life. I've produced an amazing son. One that I'm so fucking proud of. Do not give up your life for me."

I blinked my eyes to hold back the tears that wanted to trek down my face. I would do anything for Papa. He'd literally done everything so that I could achieve all my dreams, there was no way that I would stand back and just watch him die. No, that wasn't an option. I squeezed Papa's hand and stood from my seat. I circled the table to where he sat and opened my arms, pulling Papa into my chest.

"I love you, Papa," I said as I kissed his thinning hair.

Papa cleared his throat. "I love you too, Dill. Never forget that."

"I couldn't possibly," I replied before I let Papa go.

• • • •

(18 YEARS OLD)

My phone buzzed on the pillow beside my head. I sighed as I glanced at the screen. There was only one person that would ring me at this ungodly hour of the morning. "Harry," I groaned, "you know I was working late last night."

Harry, my boss chuckled. "I'm sorry Dylan. I have a job that I thought you might like."

"If it is for the football club again, never, never again. They were a bunch of oafs with the manners of fucking pigs," I growled.

Harry barked out a laugh. "I'm sorry, I did warn you that they were assholes."

"Yeah, you never warned me that they'd be grabby assholes. Shit, I was a waiter for fucks sake, I was completely dressed."

"Yeah, I'm going to have a word to Bradley about their behavior. I've had a few complaints this morning from the other waiters. I'm sorry about this."

I sighed. I couldn't really complain. Harry was a fantastic boss. He'd given me the job on the spot when I rang him and showed up for an interview. He knew I had no waiting or catering experience, but he was prepared to give me a go so that I could help my Papa out. Papa's chemo took a lot out of him, and our bills had piled up. I earned enough to cover our house payments and living expenses, but beyond that, there wasn't much left. That meant his medical bills stacked up. I'd been working more and more jobs just to make ends meet.

Harry did what he could for me. But until Papa's cancer was gone, I was just going to have to push through.

"So, what do you want me to do?" I asked.

"Well, now, look, if you want to say no to this, I will totally understand, it's just that Flynn broke his leg and can't."

I knew exactly where this was going. Flynn was a dancer or stripper in the truth of the matter. He did private parties. The rules were that he wasn't to be touched, but occasionally I knew that Flynn took extra money from rich alphas to let them fuck him or to suck their dick. It was something that Harry didn't approve of but turned a blind eye to. I didn't know much of Flynn's story, but I knew that he struggled for money, as much as I did.

"Who is the job for?" I asked.

"The Devil's Advocates. That's why I said yes to the job. If it had been for anyone else, I wouldn't have asked you, but I know these guys. They are good people, they won't be grabby, and they obey all the rules," Harry explained.

I knew of the Devil's Advocates. I'd seen them riding around Lalbert and the truth was, most of the crew were hot as fuck. I wouldn't mind getting my hands on some of them that were for sure.

"Yeah, alright. I'm game. I'll do it," I replied.

"Thank you, Dill. I will be tripling your payment for this job," Harry said.

I gasped and my eyes widened. This couldn't have come at a better time. Triple the pay would allow me to pay off a huge chunk of Papa's medical bills. It might catch us up a bit.

"Thanks, Harry. When do I need to be ready?"

"Next Saturday, it's the twenty-first birthday of twins, Jai and Jasper."

I nodded my head and noted down everything that Harry told me. He said that he would have a uniform for me, all I would need to do was to come up with a dance routine. Apparently, Flynn was willing to help me out, but Harry said that the dancing didn't matter so much, I just had to grind over the guys. It sounded easy and something I could do.

Chapter One

J ai

I sat in the tattoo chair at Shifter Ink while Brenton's tattoo gun buzzed. I loved the feel of the needle in my skin. Tattoos were my addiction. I'd been getting them since I was fifteen years old. My first tattoo was done with a homemade prison job that I and my brother Jasper had rigged up. It was the worst tattoo and ended up getting horribly infected, but it was also my favorite. After Anghus and Lynx saw the state of it, they took me to a tattoo artist and signed the paperwork to let me get work done before I turned eighteen.

Since that day I'd been adding more and more art to my body. Today's artwork was the reaper and sickle crest of the Devil's Advocates. We were about to celebrate our twenty-first birthday. Even though we had, had to grow up early due to our life with Morpheus, it felt like our twenty-first birthday was a line in the sand that said we had arrived. We were now adults.

That morning, Anghus and Lynx had called the community together where Jasper and I were gifted our new cuts. We were no longer prospects. Turning twenty-one meant that we were about to become a full-fledged Devil. It also meant that it made room for more prospects. Walker was gifted his cut. His family was cheering him on. Donte was also brought in as a prospect. And Vaughan who had been in trouble finally came off his probation and was given the chance to prospect once more.

This meant it was time to celebrate. Jasper and I would be having a party on Saturday night. I didn't know what was planned. But it had been hell the last few years. With this war that was impending, the Devil's hadn't had a chance to just let our hair down and party. It would be so good to throw back to the time of old. Partying in the old days meant loads of liquor, laughter, plenty of food, and dancing.

We never did the whole bring-in prostitutes things. We would regularly have dancers who came in for later in the night, but we always respected our dancers. Never were they mistreated or roughly handled. Everyone knew the rules. We showed respect. It was one of the only rules that were held firm. Anghus had been certain to keep that rule at the top of our priorities.

"There ya go, man," Brenton said as he finished the final bit of shading in the center of my chest.

I looked down at the new artwork with a grin. "Fuck, you are so talented."

Brenton chuckled. "Thanks, mate. I've been doing it a long time now."

Brenton was a vampire. I didn't know how old he was, but from what Burgess had said, he was old. I glanced over the studio to where Jasper was getting his tattoo. He looked up at me and smiled. I signed to him that I was done, and he gave a nod of his head. The work that Jasper was getting was on his back, but Jasper the damned masochist had decided to get scarred instead from Chase.

I liked pain, but Jasper was a lot tougher than I was. He'd experienced so much fucking pain in his life. His first fight had been brutal. He never regained his hearing and in the winter his bones often ached like crazy. It wasn't anything unusual to see Jasper curled up in front of the fire during the winter with tears in his eyes. I would give anything to take it all away from him. But it was what made him who he was.

"So, what's the plan for your birthdays?" Brenton asked as he wrapped the tattoo on my chest.

"Party, party, party," I laughed.

Brenton chuckled. "Ahh, those were the days. I'm too old and tired for that now."

"Man, you can never be too old to party," I scoffed.

Brenton barked out a laugh and winked at me. "Trust me love; you'll get there one day. Enjoy being young."

"All done," I heard Chase say as he tapped Jasper on the shoulder and gave him a thumbs up.

The one thing I loved about living in Lalbert, is that almost everyone I had met, just accepted Jasper for who he was. They never treated him any different. I was fiercely protective of my brother. We went everywhere together. I was often his hearing for him. I know that he hated it, that he was reliant on me or the others. But I never felt like he was a burden. I loved Jasper. He wasn't just my brother; he was my best friend.

Jasper stood from the seat and went to the mirror, looking over his shoulder at the work that Chase had done, I watched as a smile crept across his face and he turned to give Chase a thumbs up.

"You like it?" he asked.

Jasper looked to me so I could sign what Chase had asked. Jasper could read lips, but sometimes it was hard, especially with vampires who didn't move their lips the same as others, thanks to the shapes of their mouths and their fangs.

Jasper nodded his head and signed back to me. *I fucking love it.* I chuckled and repeated to Chase what Jasper had said to him. Chase grinned and nodded his head. "Let him know that I'll wrap it for his healing to take care of the scarring and then you guys are right to go."

I signed what Chase said and Jasper nodded his head before going back over to the vampire and allowing him to wrap up the tattoo. Once we were done, we headed outside onto our bikes. This was life, bikes, tattoos, and freedom. The only thing that might make it complete might have been a mate. But I'd never admit that to anyone.

Chapter Two

D ylan
How in the holy fuck do I do a dance? I texted Flynn.

My phone rang immediately, and I looked down to see Flynn's number pop up, when I answered the phone, I was greeted with hysterical laughter.

"Alright, alright, it's not that funny," I grumbled.

Flynn snorted. "It kinda is. Have you never danced sexy before? Like heard a song that just brings out your inner stripper and shimmied around your room."

I thought about the kind of music I often listened to. It wasn't stuff that brought out the inner stripper in me. I liked heavy, loud, and angry music. It brought out feelings, but nothing sexy.

"Nope. I don't listen to music that brings out an inner stripper," I answered.

Flynn sighed and I could hear his exasperation through the phone. "I swear you're a strange egg, Dill. I can't drive now, can you come over to my place and I'll put you through your paces?"

I looked at the clock. I still hadn't gotten out of bed and Papa would be due for his medication. If I made sure he had something easy to eat, I knew that he would be fine until I could get back. That was why working for Harry was so good. It was night work; I was able to get Papa fed and in bed before I left and knew that he would be alright until I got back.

The chemo had taken so much out of him. He had once been a strong man, a mystical kelpie. But cancer and chemo had wreaked havoc on his body. He was now so thin and weak. I worried about him and often thought that he would do better with a nurse to come in for him, but there just wasn't the extra money to be able to afford such things.

"Yeah, I can come out, I just have to get Papa up and fed, clothed, and set up and then I can be there around lunchtime?"

"Sounds good. Take your time. Your Papa comes first," Flynn said.

I didn't let a lot of people into the struggles that I went through. But Flynn and Harry had become my confidants. They knew my story and knew why I was prepared to do the jobs I did. Once I left school all my friends that I had drifted away. But when I started working for Harry, I was able to meet Flynn and we quickly became friends. The unicorn was different in every sense of the word. He was as flamboyant as he alter. But as clumsy as they came. I worried about him sometimes as often as I worried about Papa. The problem that Flynn had was that he wasn't able to shift. So, something like a broken leg, meant he had to wait it out, just like a human. His healing was somewhat faster than a human, but it still wasn't as instant as most supernaturals who could shift.

Harry was often stressed about Flynn. Harry treated all his staff fantastically. He cared for all of us. We were more like a family than employees. But Flynn had a special place in Harry's heart. At first, I thought they might have been together, but Flynn insisted they weren't. There was more to their story, but I never pushed.

I said goodbye to Flynn and climbed out of bed, slipping into a pair of sweatpants and a t-shirt before going into Papa's room. The room was dark, and his c-pap machine was the only sound that filled the room. I walked over to the bed and noticed that Papa was still asleep. Leaving him be, I went into the kitchen and set about making him some scrambled eggs and toast for breakfast, along with a cup of tea and his morning pills.

Unfortunately, his pills that were aimed at keeping Papa alive, were the same pills that were slowly killing him. I know that he hated having to rely on me and there were times that I would hear him crying in his room and begging for the creator to take him home. It broke my heart. I wished there was more I could do for him. I wished I could take the pain away. Cancer was a cunt of a disease that I wouldn't wish on my worst enemy.

Once his breakfast was ready, I set it up on the table that sat beside his favorite recliner and went back into the bedroom. When I entered his bedroom again, I saw that Papa was now awake and struggling to sit up.

"Morning, Papa," I said as I reached out and took the oxygen mask from him and placed it on the machine beside his bed.

"Morning," Papa groaned as he wrestled with the blankets to move them from his body.

I pushed open the curtains and turned back to see that Papa had managed to sit up and move his feet to the floor. His pajamas were twisted on his body from his sleep and his face was creased from the oxygen mask he wore at night.

"I made you some scrambled eggs, toast, and a cup of tea, they are out by your chair. I'm going to go to Flynn's after I've made you some lunch and put it in the fridge. I've got a job coming up on the weekend, Flynn is going to help me with it," I explained.

Papa coughed a hacking cough and reached out for some tissues that he wiped across his mouth. I placed the walker in front of Papa and reached under his arm to help him stand. Once he was steady on his feet, I quickly straightened out his pajamas and watched him walk towards the door.

With a heavy sigh, he shuffled into the living room. I quickly made Papa's bed, so that I wouldn't have to worry about it before I left and followed him into the living room. He was just sitting in the recliner when I entered the room. I pushed the table over his lap and handed him his tablets. He swallowed them down with his cup of tea.

"Thank you, son. I wish you didn't have to do this damned job," Papa said with a sigh. His voice was harsh and raspy from lack of use.

"It's alright Papa. Harry is a good man to work for. And I am looked after," I said. It was the same thing I said every time Papa brought up my job. He would have liked to see me go onto university and become something greater than a personal waiter and now dancer. I knew that, but there was never going to be a chance that I would have left Papa behind when he needed care. That just wasn't an option.

I went into the kitchen and set about making him some sandwiches that he could easily take out of the fridge to eat. Cleaning the kitchen behind me I made sure that there was nothing in the way that Papa could trip on. When I was satisfied that everything was safe to leave, I went back into the living room where Papa was finishing the last of his scrambled eggs.

"Do you want to get dressed today?" I asked.

Papa shook his head. "No. I think I'm going to go back to bed. I'm tired."

I smiled but kept the sigh inside that wanted to escape. He had been sleeping a lot more often lately, which was making me nervous. I couldn't help but feel we were getting very close to the end.

"Alright, want to have a shower and change your pajamas to fresh ones before you hop into bed?"

Papa shook his head. "No. I haven't got the energy today. I'll have a wash later maybe. You go and have fun with Flynn. I will be fine."

I sighed and nodded my head. Papa gave me a weak smile and started his slow shuffle back to his bedroom. I followed behind him and closed the curtains as he maneuvered himself into bed. I reached over the bedside table and handed him the remote for the television that I'd had installed and made sure that his phone was beside him.

"You call me if you need me, don't you dare ignore it," I said with a fake glare.

Papa smiled and nodded his head. "Yes Papa," he said with a small chuckle.

I grinned and leaned down pressing a kiss to the top of Papa's head as he flicked the television onto the news programs that were the only thing he could tolerate watching.

"I love you, son," Papa said as I turned to leave the room.

Tears burned in my eyes. *Why did it feel like this was the end?*

"I love you too Papa," I said after clearing my throat. "I'll see you when I get home."

Papa nodded his head and closed his eyes. I stood watching him for a few more moments before turning and leaving the house. Worry filled my chest and I considered canceling on Flynn. *But what could I do?* If it was time for the creator to take him, I wasn't going to stop it from happening. That had been Papa's only request, I was not to resuscitate him. It had caused a lot of tears when he'd had that discussion with me. I rejected the idea immediately. But in the end, I'd given in. Papa never asked much of me, the most I could do was honor him in death.

Chapter Three

I drove to Flynn's house with worry floating through my mind. I almost found myself turning around and going home several times. If the money wasn't such a great help, I might have rung Harry and told him I couldn't do this job.

By the time I got to Flynn's house, I'd been practically frantic with worry for Papa. I pulled out my phone and chewed on my lip. Scrolling through the contacts I found Papa's number and pressed on it, before bringing the phone to my ear and listening to it ring.

"Did you forget to tell me something, son?" Papa answered with amusement in his voice.

"I was worried about you and wanted to make sure you were alright?"

Papa chuckled before it turned into a hacking cough and I could hear him shuffling in the bed, reaching for his tissues. "I'm fine, Dylan. You've literally been gone fifteen minutes. I'm fine. I'll be fine. Spend time with Flynn. Be a kid for a while. You are only eighteen years old. Enjoy that time."

I sighed and scrubbed my hand up over my face. "Sorry, Papa. I'm just worried about you. I think we need to go back and see Dr. Rankin again; I'm worried at how tired you are."

Papa sighed. "Son, this is just part of this disease. We knew that one day it was going to kill me. I don't like it. I know you don't like it. But unfortunately, that is part of having cancer."

I felt my eyes burning with tears. I hated it when Papa spoke about his death like it was normal. He was only fifty-three years old. Not old enough to be dying. Being a shifter, we typically lived a lot longer than humans. Papa hadn't even reached middle-aged yet.

"Be a kid for a bit Dylan. Fuck knows, you deserve the break," Papa said.

"I don't want the break. I want my Papa," I said with a small sob.

"I know baby, I know. I wish that this wasn't our lot. I wish a lot of things hadn't been your lot. But we can't stop fate, love."

I sighed. "I know Papa. Thank you for being the Papa you have been. I wouldn't be half the man I am today without you."

Papa chuckled. "You will continue to grow and be a wonderful man. I know that for sure."

"Oh yeah? You psychic now?" I laughed.

"I've got eyes everywhere," he said with a smile in his voice. "Go and have fun. I'm going to just have a nap and then eat those sandwiches you made me. I'll be still here when you get back."

I smiled, but it was a smile that felt like anything other than joy. "Okay, Papa, remember to ring me if you need me."

"I will son," Papa promised before he ended the call. My stomach was still clenched with worry, but I felt better after speaking to Papa. I knew that the day that I would lose him was very close. I just wanted him to hold on for a little longer.

I climbed out of the car and knocked on Flynn's door. I could hear him swearing and calling something a fuck face as he stumbled his way to open the door. His bright smile filled the doorway as it swung open.

"Hey, how's Papa?" he asked.

I shrugged my shoulders and went in through the door as Flynn moved out of the way with his crutches. "I don't think he has long left now," I admitted.

Flynn winced and sighed. "I'm sorry Dill. You don't deserve that."

I shrugged my shoulders and ran my hands up over my face as I looked around Flynn's living room. The place looked like a tornado had swept through it.

"What on earth is going on in here?" I asked. Flynn wasn't someone who was considered clean and organized. His house always had chaos in it, but it was at least slightly controlled. Now, however, it was like a bomb had been set off. Dishes, clothes, empty bottles, and cans spilled over every surface.

Flynn sighed. "This stupid fucking leg. I can't fucking do anything without using the crutches, which makes cleaning a million times worse."

"Why didn't you say something, I would have come around and helped you," I scolded.

Flynn frowned and shook his head. "Dill, you have enough on your plate with your Papa. I wouldn't expect you to come and look after me too. That's not fair."

I shrugged my shoulders. "It's not like it's forever, it would only be until you got your cast off. How the hell did you break your leg anyway? I didn't even know until Harry told me this morning."

Flynn huffed. "I'm not telling."

"Oh dear," I said knowing that it was something that he was doing that would be considered stupid.

"Look it wasn't my fault I didn't see the gutter and I was practicing wearing my new heels."

I winced. "Ouch."

"Yeah. I looked like a two-bit fucking hooker sitting in the gutter with seven-inch heels on and a wig falling off my head and my makeup running." I ran my hand over my mouth to hide the smirk that was forming on my lips. Flynn rolled his eyes. "Yeah, yeah, laugh it up. Asshole," he huffed at me.

"Come on, let me help you at least clean up the living room so I've got room to shimmy and dance for you and you can give me some pointers," I said as I started to collect the pile of dishes off the coffee table and take them to load them in the dishwasher. Looking around I noticed that the rest of the house wasn't as bad as the living room.

"Who is the party for anyway?" Flynn called as he sat down on the couch and started to throw clothes into a pile of dirty and clean.

"The Devil's Advocates," I replied as I grabbed a garbage bag and started to fill it with empty bottles of water.

"Oh, you fucking lucky cunt. I'd give anything to get my hands on one of those guys," Flynn said. "Especially that vampire with dark hair that rides with the inner Devil's."

I shrugged my shoulders. I didn't know their names. I knew the president was Anghus, but I also knew that he was mated with kids. Harry said that the party was for twins Jai and Jasper. That was the extent of my inner knowledge.

Chapter Four

J ai

As we pulled into the guard house, I noticed that Vaughan was standing guard. I frowned and pulled my bike up to a stop.

"What's going on?" I asked. Usually, we always had a fully pledged member at the guard house, not a prospect.

"Ettore was here," Vaughan answered and signed for Jasper. That was one thing I loved about Anghus, he insisted that all members learn sign language. His opinion was that it wasn't just for Jasper's sake but the possibility that some of the omegas we got were more comfortable to speak in sign rather than use their voices.

"Shit," I spat. "What the fuck happened?"

"He dropped Brooklyn at the guard house, Miles was on guard, he rushed her through to the medical unit and Anghus called me to stand guard until someone could take over."

I nodded my head and glanced at Jasper who revved his bike to life and took off up the path. I rolled my bike over to the side of the guardhouse and stepped off. Vaughan looked like he was about to take off. He still wasn't sure how to act around us since his dressing down that he took after the incident with Miles's mate Freya.

"You can stay man," I said. "I was just gonna sit with you."

Vaughan nodded his head and rubbed at the back of his neck. "Look Jai, I know I fucked up in the past, but I'm really trying to make a right step forward."

I smiled and nodded my head. "I know you are man. That's why Anghus put you through as a prospect. He wants to give you a chance. You've obviously been proving to Anghus and Lynx that you've been doing the right thing."

Vaughan sighed and sat down on the seat beside me. "Yeah. I've been seeing the therapist and getting help for my anger. I know that I fucked up when I hit Freya. I know it wasn't her fault for what happened to me as a kid. I was," he said with a shake of his head. "I'm still so fucking angry."

I nodded. "I get you. I was in Morpheus too, man. I had to fight until I was thirteen. I've killed, fucking countless other supernaturals. It makes me fucking sick to think about it. I hate it. I hate them."

"But you don't seem angry?"

I shrugged my shoulders. "I am. I'm fucking livid. I want to tear Ettore's fucking fairy wings right out of his back and feed them to him. I want to torture him to a slow and painful death. I just channel that anger and hatred in the right direction. At Ettore."

Vaughan sat back in his seat and hummed. "I get it. That's what Alexandria has been trying to teach me. To channel my anger into something else."

I nodded. "You need to find a way to release the anger, safely."

"How do you do it?"

I chuckled. "I get artwork on my body, and I masturbate furiously."

Vaughan coughed out a laugh and shook his head. "Well, I've got the masturbating furiously down pat."

I chuckled. "Yeah, most guys learn that one fairly early on."

Vaughan nodded before reaching into his pocket and pulling out a packet of cigarettes, he took one out of the packet and slipped it into the corner of his lips before lighting up and inhaling deeply.

"I don't know if that girl is gonna make it," Vaughan said as he stared out at the forest that surrounded the community.

"Brooklyn?" I asked.

Vaughan nodded his head. "Yeah. She looked like she was drugged with something. Her pupils were the size of saucers, and she could barely walk. She was just speaking a lot of gibberish that no one could understand."

"Shit," I said with a shake of my head. "Hopefully Larissa will be able to help her."

"Yeah, they were calling in Arcadia and Merza to see if they could help. But with Ettore who the fuck knows what kind of magic he has used on her."

I sighed and ran my hands up over and through my hair. "Yeah, the sooner that cunt is dead the better."

"I agree. Do you think that the kids are honestly going to be able to do it?"

I shrugged my shoulders. "With the help of the gods they will. I just hope that they have enough time to grow up first."

Vaughan nodded his head. "I hope I'm still alive so I can help them fuck him up."

"Me too, man. Me too."

Chapter Five

D^{ylan} Once we had space in the living room I stood in front of where Flynn sat. "Alright, we first need to find you a song that you find sexy," Flynn said as he grabbed his phone and started scrolling. "What's your favorite song?"

"Sacrifice by Death Decline," I answered.

Flynn frowned. "Alexa, play Sacrifice by Death Decline."

The starting riff sounded through the speakers that surrounded Flynn's living room. His eyes widened and his mouth dropped open. "Alexa stop." The music cut off and Flynn shook his head. "You cannot strip to that."

"I know, that's why I came over here to get you to help me to find a song and how to do this," I whined.

Flynn chuckled. "Alright, alright, I've got one. You like rock, let's take it back to old school. Alexa, play Tainted Love by Marilyn Manson."

I smirked. Okay, I knew this song and I could strip to it. The starting beat sounded and reverberated through my chest.

"Close your eyes and move your body like you would dance, without anyone watching," Flynn said.

I blinked my eyes closed and listened to the beat of the music. The bass pulsed through my body. I felt my body starting to move in time with the music. I envisioned Tom Hardy sitting watching me as I started to move my hips. I lifted my hands and started to move them down my body before slowly moving them up over my chest to my neck and thrusting them into my hair. I continued to move my body in time with the music, allowing everything to drift away from me other than me and the sexy feeling that was washing over me.

By the time the song came to an end, I blinked my eyes open to see Flynn staring at me with wide eyes.

"Was it alright?" I asked.

"Was it alright?" Flynn said breathlessly before pointing at his cock. "I'm fucking hard as steel."

I laughed and shook my head. "Who is going to take care of that for you?" I purred, feeling my own cock stir. Flynn and I hadn't played before, but the chemistry between us was always there.

Flynn's eyes flared and he licked over his bottom lip. Wordlessly, with the next song playing, he reached down to the front of his sweats and dipped his hand inside. Slowly he started to stroke up and down his length. My cock pulsed and a small groan fell from my lips. Who thought sexy dancing could turn into making the dancer feel so fucking horny.

"Sit down in the chair opposite me. I want to watch you jerk off," Flynn said with a husky voice.

I nodded my head and sat in the chair that we had previously pushed against the wall. I took the waistband of my sweats and wrestled them down my legs, along with my boxers. My cock was hard and weeping. Flynn watched my movements and wrestled with his own pants. His cock wasn't as thick or long as mine, but it was just as hard and weeping a steady stream of pre-cum.

I stroked my hand up over my shaft and circled the head. I lifted my palm to my lips and licked the underside of my hand before moving it back to my shaft. In my other hand, I held my balls and ran my fingers down over my taint to my hole. I wasn't a virgin but hadn't spent a lot of time being a bottom. I'd topped a few times and bottomed a handful of times but had only ever been with other omegas.

"Fuck that is hot," Flynn moaned.

I bit into my bottom lip as my toes curled in my socks. I sped up my movements as I stroked my cock in time with Flynn. He groaned and thrust his hips up into his hand.

"I'm going to cum, Dill, cum with me," he moaned.

I nodded my head and kicked my sweats and boxers off my feet before I lifted my legs onto the arms of the chair. I slid two fingers down over my crack and circled my hole. Flynn gasped as I slid a finger inside me. My eyes rolled as my finger slid over my prostate. I pressed in a second finger and felt my hole pulse around me.

"Open your eyes, Dylan, I want to see them when you cum," Flynn demanded.

I shot my eyes open and stared into my friend's face as I continued to stroke my cock in one hand while the other pressed on my prostate. My breath was coming out in pants. My balls drew up tight and my toes curled.

"Fuck," I roared as jets of cum hit my stomach.

Flynn cried out as he followed me over the edge. He looked over at me and a small smirk formed on his lips.

"Why, Dylan, you are a dirty, dirty boy," he chuckled. "And I have the perfect song for you to strip to."

"Yeah?" I replied. "Better than Marilyn Manson?"

Flynn nodded his head. "Alexa, play Rev 22:20 by Puscifer," he called.

The song switched over and the slow beat of the song Flynn requested started to play through the speakers. I groaned and closed my eyes. Yeah, this would work. Fuck, this would so work. My cock started to stir at the very thought.

Flynn chuckled and I opened my eyes. "Yep. This is the song." Flynn grinned and nodded his head. "Whoever you are dancing for is going to be one very fucking lucky person."

I grinned. "Hopefully they are hot," I laughed.

"That's a high likelihood, I've not seen an ugly Devil yet."

Chapter Six

J^{ai}

I found sitting and talking to Vaughan that he was a complex guy. I wondered how many people had just looked at him and seen a troll and cast him off as a meathead. But in fact, he was a man with an intricate brain who thought and felt deeply. He told me that he felt miserable about hitting Freya and was sorry he'd done it. Freya forgave him but had chosen not to have anything to do with him.

I didn't know a lot about Freya's story, but from what Vaughan told me she was his protector when he was little, and he was so angry that she'd never come back for him, but he now understands that she didn't have a choice. His story was heartbreaking. But it resembled virtually every kid that had the misfortune of being born or taken by Morpheus. Mine and Jasper's life was the same. Filled with beatings, starved, and mistreated. I was one of the lucky ones that weren't raped. But it sounded like Vaughan, and I know Jasper wasn't so lucky.

Once Jasper could no longer fight, our Morpheus handlers took their sexual frustration out on him. The reason for the scarification on Jasper's body was to hide the scars that our Morpheus owners had caused. He didn't like to talk about it, and I didn't blame him, but for a long time he would only get undressed in front of me, he didn't even trust Anghus to see him without clothes on. He kept waiting for the time that Anghus would rape him too. Obviously, it never happened, and Jasper soon started to trust everyone around him.

However, what it did was turn Jasper into a bit of a man whore. There wasn't a single woman that he didn't fuck if she wanted it. He never pushed himself on any of them obviously. But he was a good-looking guy, men and women liked him. They have always, but he never put himself in a position to be vulnerable again. He was a power top and everyone that fucked him knew it. I worried about him,

I worried that he wasn't going to find love in his life, but it was what he had chosen. It was what kept him safe.

I was still kicked back in the chair when I heard the distinct sound of Jasper's bike coming down the road. He pulled it up beside my bike and walked into the guard house.

How is she? I signed with him.

Jasper shook his head and sighed. *Not good. She has been drugged with some apparently ancient poison, but it also means that there is no known cure.*

"Fuck," I groaned as I signed for him too. "This is fucked."

Jasper and Vaughan nodded their heads. "Is she going to die?" Vaughan asked as he signed for Jasper.

Jasper nodded his head. *Yeah, it looks that way. Arcadia and Oakland are working with the ancestors to try and find a cure, but at this stage, it's not looking good.*

"What about the baby she had? Do we know where Ettore took the baby?" Vaughan asked.

Jasper shook his head. *No. Scout and the Onyx Rebels are looking for them, but it's like Ettore had disappeared off the face of the earth.*

I frowned. I hated that fuck. I wanted him dead. Fuck we all did. "Has Brooklyn been able to say anything?" I asked.

Yeah, Jasper signed. *She got pregnant again, but this time the baby was an omega. She believes that Ettore killed the baby, a little girl, and then poisoned her and left her here because he had no need for her anymore. The baby was old enough for him to start taking care of him.*

Vaughan growled and shook his head. "I hate that fucking cunt."

"Me too man," I said as Jasper nodded in agreement. Another bike sounded as it came down the driveway and when I looked up, I saw that it was Corson. He stepped off his bike and crowded into the doorway of the guardhouse.

"I'm here to take over from Vaughan. You did a good job man," Corson said as he signed for Jasper's benefit.

Vaughan smiled and I swore his chest puffed at the praise. "Thank you," he replied before ducking his head and his cheeks pinkened. The big troll stood and went to the doorway. "Thanks for keeping me company, Jai, it was really good talking to you."

"Anytime man, don't be a stranger, come hang out now and then hey?" I replied.

Vaughan's smile grew and he bounced his head up and down before he took off out of the guardhouse and jogged up the path.

"That was pretty mature man," Corson said with a wide grin.

I chuckled and shook my head. "I am capable of maturity now and then, you know," I said with a roll of my eyes making Corson laugh.

"So, you two ready for your party on the weekend?"

I glanced over at Jasper who scrunched his nose up. Jasper wasn't the partying kind; he didn't like being the center of attention.

"Is it still going to go ahead with Brooklyn being ill?" I asked.

Corson nodded his head. "Yeah, Anghus wouldn't allow you guys to miss out. This is a big deal."

I grinned and stood from the chair. "Then yeah, I can't wait to party."

Corson smiled and looked up at Jasper. *How about you?*

Jasper shook his head. *Nope. I fucking hate parties. But you never know I might get lucky and can skip out early.*

Corson chuckled and rolled his eyes. "You think too much with your dick, man," he said as he signed making Jasper laugh.

What can I say? Little Jasper likes the attention.

I bet he does, Corson signed with a laugh.

I slapped Jasper on the back and waved goodbye to Corson as I left the guardhouse and straddled my bike, kicking it to life I headed towards the main house, where I lived with Anghus, Bacchus, Joachim, and their kids. Iver was sitting on the steps with his eyes closed and his lips moving in conversation. When I stopped my bike and started up the steps, he opened his eyes and I saw that they were filled with tears. I sat down on the step beside my nephew and pulled him into my arms.

"Wanna talk about it?" I asked.

"She's gonna die, Jai," he said with a sigh. "I asked the creator to save her, but they said that she had to die so that the baby could grow his true powers."

I held Iver closer and stroked a hand down over his back. "Is the baby going to be on our side one day?"

Iver shrugged his shoulders. "I've asked, but I don't know. I hope so."

"Me too."

Chapter Seven

D^{ylan}

Every morning I got Papa up and ready for the day, he'd promised that he would call Dr. Rankin for a check-up which made me feel a little better about leaving him so that I could go over to Flynn's home and practice my routine. After our first unexpected circle jerk, our dance lesson's ended the same way. We'd come to an unspoken agreement not to touch one another, but we were happy to get off together.

By the time that Saturday night rolled around, I felt that I was well prepared for my first ever dance. I'd first dropped Flynn off at my house. He and Papa were going to spend the evening together. Dr. Rankin had visited on Friday and said that the chemo was taking more out of Papa than what had been expected. He was booked in for more scans on Monday, but I wasn't comfortable leaving him on his own. It was going to be a bigger day than normal.

Flynn said that he would order a pizza for him and Papa. I think Papa was just glad to have someone else there that wasn't fussing all over him. They were planning a night of pizza and movies. It made me feel more comfortable.

I went to the head office of Reynolds party and catering, where we were all stationed. I was meeting Harry at the office, and he was giving me the uniform that I would wear and helping me to get ready. I would then take Harry's car to the Devil's Advocates compound on the outskirts of Lalbert. I hadn't been to their compound, but Harry and Flynn assured me that I would be fine.

"Dylan, good to see you man, I hear that you and Flynn have been practicing your dance?" Harry said with a smile that made me wonder if he knew how we finished each session.

I nodded my head as a blush crept up on my cheeks, causing Harry to chuckle. He moved away from his desk and opened the locker that sat behind him. Harry pulled out a pair of red booty shorts and a matching mesh shirt.

"There isn't much to the uniform as you can see," Harry said holding it up, before bending to pick up a pair of boots that my Papa would have called shit-kicker boots. "I've got some body glitter for you too."

"Won't the glitter come off?" I asked as I thought about sweat.

Harry grinned and winked. "That's the idea," he chuckled. "The Devil's Advocates are good people. They have a good set of morals and won't touch you. But if you want to get laid, then that's on you."

I shook my head. "No, I'll just dance. I need to get home to Papa."

Harry nodded. "How is your Papa doing?"

I sighed and shrugged. "Not great. We have more scans on Monday, but Dr. Rankin said that he isn't holding out hope that the cancer has gone away or that the chemo is even working."

Harry winced. "Shit, I'm sorry, Dill. I will do whatever I can to help. If you need extra work or an advance, just say so."

I sighed and smiled. "Thank you, Harry. This job will help a lot with catching up on medical bills."

Harry nodded his head and lifted the uniform off his desk and handed it to me. "Get dressed and then come back in here, I'll glitter you up."

"Thanks," I murmured as I took the uniform and went into the staff bathroom. I stuffed my sweats and shirt into my backpack. Looking at the little booty shorts, I wasn't going to be able to wear underwear beneath without showing the lines. I'd brought a jock strap to wear beneath but at the last minute decided to leave it off.

Once the shorts were on, I looked at myself in the mirror, adjusting myself to make my bulge look right, turning back and forth I took myself in at different angles. I smiled. I felt sexy. I slipped the mesh shirt over my head and let it fall. It was loose on my body. My nipples perked up as the material brushed over them. I almost wished I had my nipples pierced. But that was a thought for another day.

I wasn't muscular like Flynn was, but I had a good body too. I was thin, but firm, just not bulky. I thought I looked good anyway. I slipped the boots on and took my backpack with me to Harry's office. Harry looked up at me as I entered, and he grinned.

"Looking sexy," he said with a wiggle of his brows.

I laughed and shook my head. "Alright boss, glitter me up."

Harry chuckled. "Take the shirt off, we will glitter your chest and back and then face."

I nodded my head and slipped the mesh shirt off my body and stood with my arms out as Harry proceeded to dust me with gold and red glitter until I was sparkling under the lights.

"Right, got the music?" Harry asked once I slipped my shirt back on. I nodded my head. Harry reached into his pocket and pulled out his keys and handed them to me. "Keep in contact, but you will be fine."

"Thanks, Harry," I replied as I turned and went to where Harry parked his BMW in the back carpark and slipped into the driver's seat. I took a deep breath and nodded my head. I was nervous, but I was doing this for Papa. No matter what happened, it was for Papa.

Chapter Eight

J ai

I was bouncing with excitement for the party. It had been a horrible week. Iver was right, Brooklyn passed away in the early hours of the night, two days after she was dropped at the guard house. Landon her brother was devastated. She had lost consciousness after Arcadia, Merza and Oakland cast wards over her to take away any pain that she was feeling. She was awake long enough to tell Landon that she'd called her son Mormo, then she'd slipped into a coma and took her last breath the following day.

I'd offered Israel to cancel the party, but Israel and Landon both insisted that we go ahead with it. They said that we needed something good to focus on. Scout discovered that Ettore was held up in the old Morpheus training center with over three hundred alphas that no one knew where they came from, other than that they had been bred.

We hadn't heard any more about it. The Onyx Rebels were working closely with the AJE authority, but we'd been told to be prepared that the war may be coming sooner than we thought. Although Iver was insistent that it wasn't time yet. He talked a lot about Mormo, needing to come into his powers, but we still didn't know whether the demon baby was going to be on our side or not. All in all, it was a lot of uncertainty that made my stomach nauseous at the thought. I wasn't sure that I wanted to bring a child into such an uncertain world. But I also trusted in Mother fate. If she had someone out there for me, I would never deny it.

Are you ready to party? I signed to Jasper with a wide grin. Jasper rolled his eyes and chuckled but shook his head. I hmphed as I flopped into the seat beside him. *What's going on with you? You've been more miserable than usual lately. Your glare is starting to rival Anghus's.*

Jasper sighed and shrugged his shoulders. *I've just got shit on my mind.*

Wanna talk about it?

Jasper shook his head. Sometimes Jasper could be so open, but then other times he locked up until he was ready to say anything. I knew that something was bothering him, but I didn't know what it was. And I wouldn't know until he was prepared to speak about it. I slung my arm around my brother's shoulder and pressed a kiss on his cheek.

Did you invite any pretty omegas? I signed making Jasper laugh.

Of course, I did, he replied making me laugh.

Anghus came in through the door with a smirk on his lips. "You two ready?" he asked. I narrowed my eyes into a glare. My brother was planning something, he never looked as suspicious as he did at that moment.

"What have you done?" I asked. I glanced over at Jasper who was watching him with the same distrust that I had.

Anghus laughed and shook his head as he signed the same time he spoke. "Nothing. Well, nothing that you both won't like."

"Give us a clue?" I asked.

Anghus laughed again and shook his head. "Nope. You'll have to come to your party to find out."

I leaped out of my seat and bounced up and down, turning I reached out a hand and pulled Jasper out of the seat he was in. Jasper chuckled at my enthusiasm. I trusted Anghus implicitly and knew that he wouldn't have done anything that put me or Jasper in any kind of danger. We were both well protected there. Anghus took his role as president and big brother seriously. He was an amazing protector. Not to mention that we discovered what it was to be loved unconditionally. It had been strange when we first got here.

"Alright, let's go," I said, pulling Jasper along behind me and heading over to the main hall where we'd been banned from entering before the party was ready. It had been hell to try and stop from going over there to sneak a peek.

Anghus laughed and followed along behind us as I dragged Jasper with me. When we got to the main hall, I could already hear the heavy bass of the music that was playing, and I could smell the beautiful aroma of fresh meats being barbecued.

"Happy birthday, you two," Larissa said with a wide grin as we passed through the doors. She held her arms out and pulled us into a tight hug, pressing a lipstick kiss on both of our cheeks.

"Thank you, Larissa," I said before kissing her back.

"Oi, unhand my mate," Corson growled with no heat in his voice from the other side of the room. I looked up at him and poked my tongue out before taking Larissa in my arms and dipping her low, pressing another kiss on her cheeks. Larissa giggled and the men that stood around the room cheered, all slapping Corson on the back with laughter. Corson rolled his eyes and shook his head at my antics.

"Come on, Casanova, let's get you in there so that we can get this party started," Larissa said with another laugh, taking me by the hand and leading me and Jasper into the main hall where there were kegs of beer lined up on top of the bar.

Vaughan stood behind the bar with Dorian and was pouring glasses of alcohol, while, Trudy, Lucy, and a few of the other women placed heaped plates of food on long trestle tables. The music filled the room and the kids danced on a makeshift dance floor. I watched as Iver pulled out some impressive moves in front of his new best friend, Lily.

Jasper and I greeted our friends and family with hugs and kisses while they all wished us a happy birthday. I was floating on cloud nine. After years of uncertainty as a kid, I wasn't even sure that I would make it to twenty-one, but here I was. Celebrating with my twin brother and best friend by my side. My Mama and Papa standing on the sidelines watching with my two brothers and little sister. I couldn't imagine life getting any better.

Chapter Nine

D ylan

I followed the GPS in Harry's car until I reached the turn-off to the Devil's compound. I was greeted by a giant grim reaper on a metal sign that read Devil's Advocates. Slowing down as I reached what appeared to be a guard house, I couldn't see any other buildings. A tall thin man, with bright blonde hair, stepped out of the guard house and bent down to look in the car as I rolled down the window.

"Hey," he said with a grin. His green eyes sparkled, and I could tell from his scent that he was a fae. "You must be Harry's dancer."

I nodded my head. "Yes. I'm Dylan," I introduced.

"Nice to meet you, Dylan, I'm Kenji. Jasper is going to love you," he said with a chuckle.

I shook my head. Unsure what to expect and hoping like anything that Harry was right when he said that the Devil's had high morals. Kenji seemed to be able to read the look on my face and shook his head.

"You are safe here, don't stress. Jasper is one of the birthday boys, but he is a bit of a man whore, and has a very keen interest in pretty boys and girls. You fit in the category. But he won't touch you unless you ask," Kenji explained.

I let out a slow breath and nodded my head. "I'm only here to dance."

Kenji smiled again and nodded. "No stress. Right, if you follow this road straight through you will see the first big building on your left. That is the main building. A woman with bright red hair, named Freya is standing out the front waiting for you. Jai and Jasper are the birthday boys. They turn twenty-one today and don't know about you, so Freya is going to sneak you around the back until it is time to go in."

I nodded. "Alright, I can do that. Freya will be waiting?"

"Yep, she's hard to miss, just look for a red-haired vampire, dressed in leather. She may have one of her mates standing with her. You'll know them by the collars they wear," Kenji cackled.

"Alright, look for the Domme, with possible slaves," I said with a nod, causing Kenji to laugh again.

"That's the one. I'm sad I'm going to miss your dance; I wish I could see Jasper and Jai's faces when you start dancing."

I smiled and gave Kenji a quick wave before I started to edge forward towards the main building. It only took seconds before I saw the big building that Kenji was talking about. The whole area was covered in buildings, some appeared to be houses, while others seemed to be more official buildings. I was in awe and kind of wished I had time to take more notice.

I glanced at the front of the main building and saw the red-haired vampire, that Kenji called Freya standing out the front. She stood with another vampire by her side, and sure enough, looking at his neck he wore a leather collar.

When I stopped the car and climbed out Freya smiled at me and came towards me, she stuck her hand out to shake. "Hi there, I'm assuming you are Dylan?"

I nodded and shook Freya's hand. "I am, I'm assuming you are Freya."

"That's me. And this is one of my mates, Caden."

I turned and smiled at Caden, who reached out to shake my hand. "Nice to meet you, Dylan."

"You too. Kenji said that Jasper and Jai don't know about me and that you are going to sneak me around the back?"

Freya's grin grew as she nodded her head. "I am. Do you have everything you need? Music? That sort of thing?"

"Yes. I don't have any props, Harry just told me to wear this uniform and then dance," I explained.

"Oh babe, he needs some props, what about feather boas or something to wrap around the boys while he dances?" Caden suggested.

Freya's eyes lit up and she nodded. "What do you think Dylan?"

I smiled as I thought about how I could work the props into my act. "That would work. Are the boys going to be tied down or anything?"

Freya's eyes sparked and her grin grew wicked. "They are now. Baby, will you please go and bring back two pairs of hand cuffs, the feather boa, and maybe a cat of nine tails," she said to Caden before turning back to me. "You don't have to whip them, but it would be fun to maybe use the whip to just run over their bodies."

My cock gave a pulse, and I bit the inside of my lip. This was going to be difficult. "Wait, there isn't going to be any kids there?"

Freya shook her head. "No, all the kids are going to be gone by the time you go on. They are just finishing up cake and dessert now and then the parents will take the kids and those that are under eighteen out, or those that don't want to see more adult content."

I sighed a breath of relief. My brain started to fire with ideas of all the things I could possibly do. Maybe there would be time for a second song. I thought about loading Tainted Love by Marilyn Manson as a second just in case.

"Alright, let's go around the back and when Caden comes back we will be set to go. I'll handcuff the boys so that you don't have to try and work that into your routine," Freya said as she led me down the side of the main building towards the back doors.

Chapter Ten

J ai
Anghus had sent all the kids and those under eighteen off to their homes and made the announcement that if no one was wanting to witness tonight's entertainment they should think about heading home. Jasper groaned beside me, while my grin broadened. I had no idea what the entertainment was about to be, but I was all here for it.

Freya came in swinging a pair of handcuffs on her finger and smiled like a cat that just caught the canary. She beelined it for where Jasper and I were sitting. Jasper looked up and his eyes widened before he started to shake his head.

Freya tipped her head back and laughed, before tucking the handcuffs under her arm so that she could use both hands to sign with. She was a bit slower because she was still learning and sometimes it was hilarious when she got the signs mixed up and said something completely outrageous.

"I'm not going to do anything to you," she giggled as she signed for Jasper's sake. Jasper pointed at the handcuffs tucked under her arm and raised an eyebrow. "Well, these are for if you want. Obviously, if you don't want to be cuffed, then you don't have to be. But it will be fun."

Jasper shook his head. *I don't want to be cuffed,* he signed.

Freya nodded her head. *That's fine, do you want to be a part of the entertainment still?*

Jasper bit into his bottom lip before he nodded his head. While he wasn't strapped to anything he knew that he could get up and getaway at any time that he felt uncomfortable. Freya smiled and turned to me. "And you?"

"Oh yeah baby, cuff me up," I said as I thrust my wrists towards her.

Freya cackled and turned to look over her shoulder. I followed her line of sight and saw that Anghus was placing two chairs in the center of the room. Everyone had sort of moved into a circle around the chairs. I glanced over at Jasper, who seemed to visibly relax as he worked out that Anghus had obviously organized a stripper for us. It was nothing scary. Not that I thought Anghus would ever do anything to hurt us, but Jasper still lived with that deep-seated fear in his heart.

"Come on boys, come and sit on the chairs," Anghus said with a twinkle of mischief in his eye.

I sprung out of the seat I'd been sitting in and jogged into the center, flopping down into the seat that Anghus had set up. "Damn someone is keen," Lynx laughed with a shake of his head.

"Always, Lynx, always," I replied.

Once Jasper was sat beside me, Freya took one of my hands in hers and locked the cuff around my wrist before snapping the other side to the leg of the chair. I looked down and realized that she had purposely left it so that if I wanted to, I just had to knock the chair over and I could slip the cuff off the leg.

"Alright guys, as was tradition for all the inner Devil's on their twenty-first birthday, we have prepared a very nice surprise for you both. Now I don't need to remind you, that you need to show restraint and respect," Anghus said.

I rolled my eyes. We had been given that speech just about every other month for as long as he had custody of us. Anghus smiled and nodded his head as the lights were dimmed until there were just a few low lights that lit up the floor in front of us.

A bass beat filled the room and I looked around to see what would happen. The crowd parted and an omega dressed in a pair of booty shorts and a mesh top came striding into the center of the room. Suddenly my eyes widened, and my chimera let out the loudest roar I'd ever heard him make.

The omega gasped and stood still as the music continued to play. The omega looked like he was trying to sway and ignore the scent that surrounded us, but there was no mistaking it. This omega was my mate. I stood and sent the chair flying backward. My alpha needed him. Jealousy surged through me as I thought about any of the other unmated alpha's touching my mate.

My lip curled into a snarl as I ran towards the omega. Somewhere in the back of my mind, I knew that I had to stop myself. But my alpha was too close to the surface. I grabbed hold of my mate by the arms and flung him up and over my shoulder as I prepared to run out of the room with him.

"Jai, stop, now," Anghus's voice roared through the room. I felt my entire being shake under the weight of his alpha. I had no choice but to obey. I stood still while the omega was still flung over my shoulder. "Put the omega down."

Gently I stood the omega down in front of me and looked into his face. He was looking up at me with wide fearful eyes. His lips were popped open and his whole body was trembling. I'd done that. I winced and felt my body begin to crumble. I stumbled back and turned, running from the room. I pushed through the throngs of people as my cheeks heated with embarrassment and shame. Tears burned in my eyes as I dashed down the stairs and headed for my bike. I pushed hard on my muscles and felt the handcuff that was still strapped to my wrist snap, falling to the ground.

"Wait," I heard a small voice call out. If it had been anyone else's voice, I would have ignored it, but it was my mate's voice. I didn't know how I knew, but something inside me just knew. I stopped and turned to face the omega who I'd just manhandled. He jogged down the stairs and came to stand in front of me. "You're my mate."

I blinked my eyes and nodded my head. "I'm sorry," I whispered over the lump that was in my throat. "I'm sorry that I touched you like that."

The omega shook his head. "I'm not upset by that. I was a little surprised, but not upset. What is your name?"

"Jai. What's yours?"

"Dylan," he said with a smile that lit up his whole face. He was beautiful. The most beautiful man that I'd ever laid eyes on. And he was mine. "So, are you going to run away from me? Or can we get down and dirty?"

I barked out a laugh and shook my head. I reached out my fingers and stroked them down over his cheek. "Let's get down and dirty."

Dylan grinned and nodded his head as he slipped his fingers into the waistband of my jeans and stood on his toes to press a kiss to my lips. I groaned and thrust my hands up into his hair, as I pushed my tongue between his lips, to tangle with his.

"Take me to your room, Jai," Dylan said breathlessly as he broke the kiss. I took him by the hand and without another thought, I led him over to the mating quarters, that I knew would be empty.

Chapter Eleven

D ylan
It had taken a moment for my brain to catch up to what the hell was going on. I'd pushed through the crowd to start my routine when the most intoxicating scent surrounded me. My kelpie roared in my head, *mate, mate, mate.* I hadn't known which of the two good-looking men sitting in the seats it was. Well not until Jai had literally stood and swung me up over his shoulder.

When he dropped me after the huge man let his alpha rip through the room, my brain had finally caught up. But just as my mind caught up, Jai was dashing out the door. I turned and watched him leave before turning back to the big man who was standing beside me.

"Are you alright?" he asked.

I nodded my head. "That is my mate."

The big man chuckled and nodded his head. "Yes, it seems that way."

"But he is running away," I said with horror.

"He is," the big man replied with amusement.

"I've got to stop him. He's my mate," I said again, before turning and dashing out the door that Jai had run through. When he stopped and turned to face me, I could see the shame on his face. He was embarrassed at manhandling me, but it wasn't something that bothered me. Hell, I liked a little caveman-style fucking now and then.

Now I was following my mate to his bedroom, my cock was throbbing in my pants that felt too tight. My mating heat was starting to hit, and I could feel the need to be filled turning into desperation. Finally, Jai swung a door open and flipped a light. The room was literally a giant bed, with a small kitchenette and bathroom to one side. It was a little like a motel room.

"This is the mating room. It doesn't get used often, but my bedroom is in the main house, I live with my brothers there. I wanted to do this without them being able to hear," he chuckled and blushed.

I grinned. "It's great. I can moan here without worry about being heard."

Jai grinned and stroked his fingers up over my arms. "Do you moan?"

I smiled and bit into my bottom lip, nodding my head. "I like to vocalize my pleasure."

Jai hummed in his throat and bent forward, pressing his lips against mine. He swept his tongue into my mouth. I clutched at his shirt, under the leather vest that he wore. Beneath his shirt, I could feel the hard muscles that came from working hard and being a supernatural, alpha.

Breaking the kiss, I looked up at Jai. "What kind of supernatural are you?" I asked. I could scent that he was a shifter but didn't know what kind.

"I'm a chimera. What are you?"

"Kelpie."

"We are both mysticals," Jai gasped. I nodded my head and gave him a smile. "Do you want children? Because our children are going to be very powerful."

I chuckled and nodded. "I do want children."

Jai hummed again and pressed kisses over my neck and cheeks. "I'm going to like putting children in you."

I groaned as his hands roamed down over my hips and grasped my ass. My cock was impossibly hard, and I could feel my slick filling my shorts. I reached my hands up to Jai's shoulders and pushed the leather vest down his arms. Jai let me go long enough to slip it off and lay the vest on the chair beside the bed. He reached out to the hem of my shirt and slipped it up over my head. I copied his movements and did the same to him.

Silently we stripped each other of our clothes and shoes until we stood naked in front of each other. Jai's eyes roved over my body, that was still covered in the glitter that Harry had poured on me. Jai's body was tight muscles and proportional everywhere. He was tattooed over most of his body. His thick cock was uncut, veiny, and weeping with pre-cum.

With a trembling hand, I took Jai's hand in mine and led him over to the bed. "Make me yours," I said as I lay on my back on the bed.

Jai smiled down at me and bent to take my ankles in his hands. He lifted my legs and circled them around his waist as he leaned over me, kissing me deeply. I thrust my hands into his hair and ground my cock against his, as he slid over my body, our pre-cum slicking the movements. I was moaning and feeling like I was floating by the time that Jai finally moved so that the head of his cock pushed against my entrance. I bore down and opened myself up for him to slide deep inside me.

Jai pushed forward and his eyes rolled as he bottomed out. I let out a long moan. "I'm sorry baby, but this is going to be fast," he whispered.

I could see that he was holding on to the edge and it pushed me so close to the edge that I thought I was going to tip over the minute Jai moved. I stroked my hands down over his back and wriggled my hips. Jai moaned and began to move in and out of me.

Soon my toes were curling, and I was gasping as I felt my incisors begin to lengthen. My kelpie was screaming in my head to make Jai ours. Just as I was about to tip over the edge of pleasure, my body took over and I leaned forward, sinking my teeth into the soft flesh of Jai's chest. His blood hit my tongue and sent me hurtling into the stratosphere.

Jai's alpha roar echoed through the room as his knot locked in place and he leaned down to answer the mating bite on my chest. We soaked in each other's bodies as slowly we returned to reality.

Chapter Twelve

J ai and I lay connected by Jai's knot as we soaked in each other. Jai's eyes flicked open, and he looked down at me. "You're mine now, and I'm yours."

I chuckled and nodded my head. "That's true. I guess we should get to know each other, huh?"

Jai barked out a laugh and nodded his head. "Yeah, we should. How old are you?"

"I'm eighteen, and I'm assuming you're twenty-one, oh happy birthday."

Jai grinned. "What a birthday present. Shit, I would've been happy with just the dance, but this is the icing on the cake."

"I can still do the dance for you some time," I replied.

Jai moaned and pressed a kiss to my lips. At first, it was just a few pecks, but then slowly he began to deepen the kiss. My cock started to fill, but before we could get carried away a knock on the door sounded.

"Jai, keep your alpha at bay," a voice called.

Jai frowned. "Anghus, what the fuck man?" Jai called back, but I could hear he wasn't angry.

"I'm sorry for interrupting, but Dylan's phone has been ringing pretty non-stop in his backpack and I thought it must be important."

My eyes widened. "Oh shit," I swore. "It's probably my Papa."

"Can I bring the phone in?" Anghus called through the door.

"Yeah, but I'm kinda stuck at the moment," Jai called back.

Anghus snorted a laugh on the other side. "Well, you wouldn't be the first guy I've seen balls deep."

Jai rolled his eyes. "Yeah, but they are your mates."

Anghus chuckled again, just as the phone started to ring again. "I'm coming in," Anghus announced as the door opened. Much to my relief, Anghus kept his eyes diverted as he quickly moved across towards the bed and held my phone out.

The phone stopped ringing just as I took it. "Thanks," I said as I looked at the phone and realized I missed a bunch of calls from Flynn.

"No worries, if you need help, let us know," Anghus replied.

"Alright, bro, as much as I love you, having you here, while my knot is in my mate's ass, is weird," Jai said.

Anghus snorted again before he turned and left the room, shutting the door behind him.

"Is everything alright baby?" Jai asked.

I shook my head. "I don't know. I've missed a bunch of calls from my best friend, who was sitting with my Papa."

I pressed on Flynn's number and placed the phone to my ear. Flynn answered immediately. "Oh Dill, thank god. I'm sorry to ring, but it's your Papa. He fainted when he went to go to the bathroom. I rang an ambulance and they've taken him to the hospital."

I gasped and felt the tears burn in my eyes. "Is he alright?"

"Yes, the paramedics thought he was dehydrated, but wanted to take him to the hospital to be checked anyway."

Panic was gripping my chest. I didn't know what to do. "How long will this take to go down?" I asked Jai, who was watching me with concern on his face.

"Wait, what to go down?" Flynn asked.

"Sorry, Flynn, I wasn't talking to you. I was talking to Jai."

"Who's Jai?"

"Um. Well, I met my mate," I said quietly.

"What the fuck? Wait, are you two locked right now?" Flynn asked with hysterical laughter.

"Yeah," I muttered.

"I'm going to ring you back," Flynn said before he ended the call. Suddenly my phone started to ring again, but this time with facetime. I opened the call and looked at my best friend with a raised brow. "Don't look at me like that. Turn the camera around, I need to see which one you got. If it's my favorite, I'm gonna spit."

I chuckled and turned the phone around to Jai, who grinned into the camera and gave a small wave.

"Oh, fuck me, Dill, you got yourself a hottie. I swear there is something in the Devil's water," Flynn gushed.

Jai laughed. "So, which one is your favorite?"

Flynn giggled. "I don't know his name. Vampire, dark hair, rides mostly with the inner crew."

Jai chuckled. "I reckon you would be talking about Arley. He is unmated you know," he replied with a wiggle of his brows.

"Sorry, I don't mean to be pushy, but how long will it take for your knot to go down?" I asked again.

Jai sobered immediately and moved his hips. I could feel his knot move, but it was a lot smaller than it had been. "It won't be long; in the next few minutes."

I nodded my head. "Flynn, I'll go to the hospital to see Papa as soon as I can move, and then I'll ring you again. Are you alright there, or do you want me to go and pick you up first?"

Flynn shook his head. "Take your time Dill, I'll be fine here. Do you mind if I crash in your bed?"

"No, that's fine. Rest. If you need me, just ring, and I'll come and get you."

"Thanks, Dylan. Take care of your Papa and now your mate. Don't worry about me."

"Flynn, I've said this before. You are my best friend. I'll always worry about you."

Flynn smiled, but the smile didn't reach his eyes. I didn't know a lot about Flynn's family life, but I knew that he had it rough growing up. Although he grew up with his family, they weren't very accepting of him. He no longer talked to his parents, and I had only ever heard him speak about one of his sisters, even though he had a few more siblings.

I ended the call and sighed. Panic started to fill my stomach. This was a disaster. As much I didn't regret mating with Jai, I worried that

I'd fucked everything up. I wouldn't get paid for tonight, I didn't do the job. That would mean extra medical bills to pay for Papa. I didn't know how I was going to do it. There was just so much. So much pressure.

Jai wriggled his hips, and I felt his knot slip from my ass. "I'm sorry baby, about our timing," he said.

I shook my head and gave him a smile. "It's alright. Will you come to the hospital with me?"

Jai bit into his bottom lip and nodded his head. "Of course."

I smiled and quickly dressed in my sweats and t-shirt that I had in my backpack and left the mating room and headed for Harry's car. I was going to have to get it back to him, I was going to have to ring Harry. Hell, if he didn't fire me for this, I didn't know what he would do. Jai climbed into the passenger seat and as soon as I brought the car to life I was heading out of the compound and towards the hospital.

Chapter Thirteen

Jai

I could feel the nervous energy pouring off Dylan as he drove towards the hospital. "Want to tell me about your Papa?" I asked.

Dylan nodded his head and cleared his throat. "He's all I have left. My Mama left us when I was just a kid and Papa chose to raise me by himself. Last year he was diagnosed with leukemia. He's been battling it since, but it's aggressive. I know he doesn't have long left, but I'm just not ready to lose him yet."

The emotion in Dylan's voice was tearing at my heart. Although I'd only just in the last eight years got to know my Papa and Mama, I couldn't imagine how much pain it would be to lose them. Even Anghus had been more like a father than a big brother. I'd be lost without any of them. I couldn't imagine how much this was hurting him.

I reached out my hand and slid my fingers over Dylan's hand. He linked his fingers with mine and glanced over at me, giving me a small smile.

"No matter what happens, I've got you. I know I can't bring back your Papa or even save him, but I will be right beside you."

"Thank you," Dylan said as a tear trekked down over his cheek. "I don't know how to do life without him. I quit school so that I could go to work and help pay for his medical bills. But now I've probably lost my job because the first time I was trusted to dance, and I found my mate."

"I'll get Anghus to talk to Harry. They have been friends for a while, I know that Anghus will make him understand."

Dylan sighed and nodded his head. "I feel like everything has just come at me; I'm feeling a little bit overwhelmed at the moment."

"Other than the fact that your Papa is in the hospital, what is the most pressing issue you have in your mind? Let me help you ease the burden a little."

Dylan looked over at me with wide eyes and opened and closed his mouth. "You really want to do that?"

"Of course, I do. I would be a shitty mate if I didn't want to halve your burdens."

"Wow," he said with a shake of his head. "I mean I appreciate it; I really do. I just never expected that you would feel that way. I don't know what I really expected of a mate, but not that."

I chuckled. "Mother fate brought you to the Devil's. We might be a motley crew that is made up of dysfunctional pasts, but we are family. We help each other. We love each other and we support each other."

Dylan let out a slow breath and squeezed my hand. "The main issue I have is the cost of the medical bills. I earn alright money, but it is only enough to keep a roof over our heads and the bills paid. It doesn't cover the cost of all his bills."

I nodded. "Alright, well if you let me, I can help you with that. I have a lot of savings."

Dylan looked over at me and shook his head. "I could never expect you to pay for the bills."

I squeezed his hand. "Baby, mates remember. You are mine and I am yours. We are now partners, which means that if you have a problem that I can help with, then I want to. Like Vanilla Ice said, if you've got a problem, I'll solve it, or something like that."

Dylan barked out a laugh that made me smile. "You so did not just quote Vanilla Ice."

I chuckled. "Get used to it baby, I'm full of wonderful quotes."

Dylan smiled and I could feel him relax slightly as we pulled into the hospital carpark. "Do you think we just go to the emergency room?"

I nodded my head. "Yeah, they will be able to find where your Papa is from there."

Dylan pulled the car into an empty car space and killed the engine. "I've got to get this car back to Harry too and pick my car up from work. I'll have to ring Harry and explain everything too."

I leaned over the center console and pressed a kiss to Dylan's cheek. "One thing at a time. I'll send Anghus a text and get him to call Harry, he will smooth things out there. He will also be able to organize one of the Devil's to bring your car to the hospital and take Harry's back."

"How the fuck did I get so lucky?" Dylan muttered.

I chuckled. "Mother fate, babe, mother fate."

Chapter Fourteen

Dylan

I couldn't even begin to comprehend what it meant to have a mate. My main concern was my Papa. My stomach was twisted with worry. It was surprisingly comforting to have Jai holding my hand as we went into the emergency room entrance. A nurse sat behind a large plexiglass screen.

"How can I help?" she asked as I approached the desk. The nurse looked Jai up and down and licked her lips. A surge of jealousy rocketed through me. *Was this something that I was going to have to get used to?*

"I'm looking for my father, Jason Ross?" I asked, pushing the irritation out of my voice. It wasn't time for jealousy.

The nurse typed into the computer in front of her and nodded her head. "He is in the recovery bay, step over to that door and I'll bring you through."

I nodded and walked towards the door that she indicated. The door swung open, and I stepped through with Jai by my side. The scent of the hospital was always the same. The antiseptic smell burnt my nostrils. The sterile white walls, devoid of any personality. The nurse was waiting for us as we reached the back of the nurse's station.

"This way," she said before turning and walking past bays of people that were waiting to see doctors. When we reached a bay that had the blue curtain pulled around it, the nurse pulled it aside and I saw my father. His face was so pale it almost matched the white blanket that lay over him. His eyes were surrounded by dark bags, and he looked so frail.

"Papa," I said with a sob.

Papa's eyes opened and he gave me a weak smile. "Congratulations, son," he said with a croaky voice. His tongue slipped over his lips. Tubes and monitors covered his body.

"This is Jai, my mate," I introduced with a smile.

Papa smiled up at Jai and reached out a shaking hand. Jai placed his hand in Papa's. "It's lovely to meet you, sir," Jai said.

Papa shook his head. "None of that sir, business. Just call me Jason or Papa."

"Thank you, Jason," Jai replied.

"What happened?" I asked.

"I just had a bit of a spill. I'm fine. I think I stood up too fast," Papa said, downplaying what had happened. I knew from the panic in Flynn's voice when he'd first answered the phone that it was more than just a bit of a spill.

"Have you seen the doctor yet?" I asked.

Papa nodded his head. "I've seen a doctor. They are just waiting for Dr. Rankin to come in. They've taken a load of blood and are planning on doing an MRI to see the state of the cancer."

My chest hurt at the thought. Papa's voice was weak, and I could see that he was struggling just to keep his eyes open. The thought that I was so close to losing my Papa, physically hurt me.

"Hello Jason," Dr. Rankin said as he came into the small cubicle about an hour later. "I hear you had a faint tonight?" Papa nodded his head and gave a small smile. "Were you dizzy before you fainted?"

"Yeah, I thought maybe I'd stood too fast," Papa replied.

Dr. Rankin nodded and breathed out heavily through his nose. "Unfortunately, your blood work has come back and it's not good. You've developed a bit of an infection. I want to do some scans to see where the infection is coming from, but I heard you coughing before I came in here, and I suspect it is your lungs."

"What can be done for the infection?" I asked.

"Well, we will start Jason on some antibiotics, but I'd also like to keep him here for a few days, with fluids, so that we can keep an eye on him."

"No," Papa growled. "I'm going to go home. You can do the tests, give me antibiotics, but I'm not staying in hospital."

"Papa please, if you are sick you need to stay here so you can get better."

Papa sighed and shook his head. "Son, I'm not getting better. It's time for me to let go, and it's time for you to live your life. You have a new mate now. You will soon have children of your own and understand that although I'd love to see them born and grow, it's just not in my lot."

Tears filled my eyes, and I shook my head. "Please Papa, I can't lose you."

"I'm sorry son, I wish I could live forever and give you everything you want, but the creator is the one that dictates when our time is to be born and when we are to be taken from the world. It's my time now."

Jai reached out and rubbed his hand over my back as a small sob fell from my lips. "Jason, I'm going to also give you a script for pain relief, I would like to make your last little while on earth as comfortable as possible. I will organize someone to come in and help you."

Papa shook his head. "No need for that. My hospital bills are expensive enough. I don't want to add to the burden I'm already leaving my son with."

"If I can suggest, the Devil's Advocates have medical people, I can organize for Larissa to come and check on Jason," Jai said.

Papa turned and smiled at my mate. "Thank you, son. I appreciate that."

This was it. My Papa wasn't going to fight anymore. He was going to give in. I was going to lose my Papa.

Chapter Fifteen

J^{ai}

While Jason was getting his scans, Dylan had called his boss to smooth things over. As it turned out he never should have bothered. I had a feeling that it wouldn't have mattered what happened, Anghus would have paid Harry regardless. It was the type of guy my brother was. Dylan explained to Harry about finding his mate and then having to be in the hospital with his Papa. Harry said he completely understood and told Dylan he was putting his pay into his account early.

Anghus had organized for Harry's car to be picked up from the hospital and Dylan's car to be returned, all we had to focus on was making sure that Jason was alright.

"Here he is," the orderly said as he wheeled Jason back into the room after undergoing his scans. Jason looked exhausted. His skin was grey and the bags under his eyes told me that this was exhaustion that went deeper than just needing sleep. He was at the end of his fight.

"It'll be alright son, no matter what the scans say, I'm going to be alright," Jason said quietly to Dylan who had his head resting on his Papa's arms.

"I'm supposed to be the one comforting you," Dylan mumbled causing Jason to chuckle slightly.

"When you have a foal of your own, you'll soon work out that no matter what is going on in life a Papa always wants to comfort and love on his children," Jason replied.

Dylan sighed and nodded his head but didn't say anything. It tore at me knowing that there was a good chance that Jason wouldn't be around to meet any of his grandchildren. From what I could tell Jason truly loved his son and took his role of Papa very seriously. I knew how much the different ones in the Devil's who were fathers were with their

"""

children. It was something that I really wanted to experience. I just wished that Jason would be around to see it.

Dr. Rankin entered the room with a serious look on his face. "Jason, I really would like it if you were to stay here for the night," he began.

Jason cut the doctor off with a firm shake of his head. "No. No more hospital stays. I want to die in my home."

Dr. Rankin sighed and scrubbed at his chin. "Alright. I can't force you to stay. The scans show that cancer has spread, the chemo is no longer going to be effective unfortunately as it has spread to your heart and lungs. I will be giving you some morphine which will help ease the pain and let you sleep."

"How long can we expect?" Jason asked.

Dr. Rankin twisted his lips. "Maybe a few weeks. It just depends on how quickly cancer attacks your heart. You are going to need to be on oxygen probably over the next few weeks, as your lungs begin to shut down. Once that happens things will move very quickly."

It shocked me at how matter of fact the conversation was. But I guessed that once someone got to this point in their mortality it was better to not blow smoke up their ass anymore and give them the facts. Jason nodded his head and stroked a hand over Dylan's back as a small sob fell from his son's lips.

Dr. Rankin glanced over at me. "You will be able to organize nursing care for him?"

I nodded my head. I'd already questioned Anghus about it in a text and he was prepared to sort everything out. Anghus had suggested moving Jason over to the compound to make things easier on Dylan, but I wasn't sure whether that was something he would be willing to do.

"Yeah, Larissa is going to come and visit every day. We will also have a couple of members who will come and stay with Jason, while Dylan must work or just give him a break," I replied.

"Good. My son needs some time off," Jason said quietly.

"I like looking after you," Dylan mumbled, not lifting his head from his Papa's chest. Jason rolled his eyes but smiled tenderly at his son. It seemed that Dylan was as stubborn as his father.

"Alright, well let me go and write up these medications. Can you please have Larissa contact me first thing in the morning to sort out exactly what she will need? I will be able to provide her with any equipment that she doesn't have available. We will be able to also get a hospital bed, through the palliative care team. As well as oxygen tanks and I.V. units."

"Yeah, I can do that," I answered.

Dr. Rankin nodded his head and sighed as he looked over at Jason. "You're a wonderful man Jason," he said with another nod before he turned and left the room.

Chapter Sixteen

D ylan
I was glad to be taking Papa home, but at the same time, I was even more worried about him. I didn't want to let him go, but after Jai had literally peeled me off my father, we got home, and I got him settled in bed.

"I will be alright, son," Papa said with a weak smile. It was going to be a comment I suspected I would hear a lot from him over the next coming days. But it was a lie. He wasn't going to be alright. He was going to die. He was going to be leaving this world.

I sighed and nodded my head, giving his hand a squeeze, I left the room and found Jai sitting on the couch.

"Oh shit, I forgot that Flynn is in my bed," I mumbled as I flopped onto the couch beside Jai and pressed my face into his chest.

Jai circled his arm around my shoulder and held me tight. "It's alright, I can sleep on the couch."

I shook my head. "No, there is enough room for all of us in my bed. Will it be alright if Flynn is there? We are just friends."

Jai chuckled and kissed the top of my head. "Of course, it will be. I've got the better looking of you both anyway."

I giggled and took Jai's hand in mine as I stood from the couch and pulled him up behind me. I still had glitter dotted on my body but was so exhausted that figured it would just have to wait until tomorrow. Flynn was curled on one side of my bed, with his leg up on cushions from the couch, when I slid in beside him, he briefly opened his eyes and gave me a small smile.

"Dill. Is Papa alright?" he mumbled.

"Yeah, he will be fine for tonight. Close your eyes and get some sleep," I said before pressing a kiss to the side of his head.

Jai slipped into the bed behind me and pulled me into his chest. I was sandwiched between my mate and best friend. It was the comfort

I needed after knowing that I was about to face something I'd hoped wouldn't come for a very long time.

· · · ·

I WOKE UP TO JAI'S body pressed against my back. His cock was hard and nestled against my ass, as his hands skimmed up and down my chest. He laid small kisses on my neck and when I turned my head, I noticed that he still had his eyes closed. I wasn't sure if he was still asleep or just enjoying the moment.

Flynn was still asleep and soft snores fell from his lips on the other side of me. I rocked my hips, grinding my ass against Jai, who moaned and tightened his arm around my chest.

"Baby, you keep that up and I'm going to want to fuck you," he whispered. I sunk my teeth into my bottom lip and rolled my hips again, enjoying the intake of Jai's breath.

Jai slid his hand down over my hip and into the waist of my sweats. His palm circled my cock and slid up and down, while I rocked my hips against Jai. I bit my lips together to stop the moans that wanted to escape. Slick dripped from me, and my hole pulsed with the promise of Jai's cock filling me.

Carefully Jai slipped my sweats down enough to expose my ass. He moved his hands and I felt him pulling his boxers down. He ran his cock along the crease of my ass, coating his shaft in my slick, before prodding it against my hole. I gasped as I felt him push forward and my hole stretch around his shaft. A groan slipped from my lips, and I shot my eyes over to Flynn who had his eyes open and a small smile on his lips.

"Don't stop on my accord," he said quietly, causing Jai to chuckle behind me.

Flynn flung the blankets off our bodies, and I saw that he was hard, with some maneuvering he managed to wrestle down his boxers and free his cock. He stroked his hand languidly up and down as he watched Jai slowly rock into me.

My eyes rolled in my head as Jai's cock pressed on my prostate over and over. My cock leaked a steady stream of pre-cum onto the sheet below me. Jai stroked his hand up and down over my shaft while sucking on the sensitive skin of my neck. Moans fell from my lips unhindered.

"Fuck that is the hottest thing I've ever seen," Flynn moaned as he stroked one hand over his nipples, squeezing each one until they were perked.

"He feels so fucking good," Jai moaned as he continued to rock inside me.

"Does it feel good Dill?" Flynn asked.

"So good."

Flynn moaned and circled the head of his cock and thrust his hips. "You're gonna make me cum soon."

Jai groaned and I felt him swell inside me. "I'm cumming baby," he growled as I felt warmth shoot deep inside me. I gasped and let out a long cry of expletives as my orgasm rocketed through my body. I could hear Flynn moaning beside me through his own pleasure.

Slowly we all came back to reality and Flynn chuckled. "Feel free to repeat that any time."

Jai barked out a laugh. "I'm sure we can make that happen again."

I chuckled. But reality had begun to sink in. I would have liked to be able to stay in bed with my mate and make love all day, but I had a role to live up to, and there was no way I could just ignore my Papa. Even for my mate.

Chapter Seventeen

Jai

I would have liked to stay with Dylan all day, but unfortunately, I was expected in at the AJE authority to help in finding what Ettore was up to. With Brooklyn dead, and the knowledge that he was holed up at the Morpheus training center, it was anyone's guess what he was planning.

Larissa had stopped in with Corson, having brought my bike over. Larissa was the only person that Corson trusted to ride his bike, so he could ride mine over. It worked out well that Larissa was coming to be the nurse for the day.

"Do you need a lift home?" I asked Flynn who was sitting on the couch while Larissa and Dylan helped Jason.

"On the back of the bike? With this?" Flynn replied as he stuck his leg out. I knew that Flynn was a shifter, and I didn't understand why he hadn't shifted to heal his broken leg but hadn't bothered to say anything. It was none of my business.

"Sure, why not? We can work it out," I replied.

Flynn sighed. "Shame that you're not Arley," he said as he glanced over at Corson who looked at me with confusion.

"Flynn has the hots for Arley," I answered the confused look on Corson's face.

Corson chuckled and shook his head. "I'm surprised it's not Jasper. That's usually who all the twinks fall for."

"Which one is Jasper?" Flynn asked looking between us.

"The deaf one, my brother," I replied.

Flynn pursed his lips in thought and shook his head. "Got a photo?"

I lifted my phone from my pocket and scrolled through my pictures. I had loads of photos of me and Jasper. I turned my phone around for Flynn to see. His eyes widened and he smirked.

"Oh yeah, he is fine. But I'm still in team Arley," he said with a laugh.

I chuckled and shook my head. "You'll have to come out to the compound and meet Arley."

Flynn shook his head and waved his hand. "I couldn't, I'd be too shy."

I folded my arms across my chest and raised a brow. "You're shy?"

Flynn chuckled and poked his tongue out at me. "Sometimes," he mumbled. "But thank you for the offer for the lift, Harry is going to come and pick me up, I needed to get some groceries and he offered."

I smiled and nodded. "All good," I replied as I turned and went to Jason's bedroom door. I rapped my knuckles on the doorframe as I looked in. Larissa was tucking him under his blankets and fluffing his pillows while Dylan stood chewing on his thumb nail with concern. Jason's face was pale still and the dark bags under his eyes seemed to look even darker.

"Hey Jai, come on in," Jason said weakly.

I stepped into the room with a smile. "How are you feeling this morning?"

"Ah, I'm alright. My son worries too much. But I have a pretty nurse to look after me, just don't tell her mate I said that."

I chuckled a laugh. "Corson would agree with you. Everyone loves Larissa."

Larissa rolled her eyes at me and waved her hand. "You behave. Right, I've spoken to Dr. Rankin this morning. The palliative care group is going to come and speak with you about bringing a hospital bed, just to make it a little easier to get you in and out of. As well as the rest of the equipment you might need."

"Are we going to have room here for that?" Jason asked.

Larissa hummed. "It's going to be a tight fit, but we should be able to make it work."

Jason sighed. "I feel like I'm such a damned burden."

Larissa shook her head. "Don't feel that way. One option we do have, if you are open to it, of course, is to move you over to the Devil's compound. There are plenty of houses available. That way you can be in a home, and we can still care for you and be able to easily fit all the equipment you need."

I knew that Anghus must have suggested the idea of moving Jason over to the compound the minute it came out of her mouth. Dylan looked over at me and then back to his father. I could see the hope in Dylan's eyes. It would make everything so much easier if Jason was willing to go with it. But it all came down to how attached he was to this house.

"Would Dylan be welcomed there?" Jason asked.

Larissa nodded. "Of course. There aren't too many people in this world that the Devils don't accept. But now that Dylan is mated to Jai, it makes him a Devil."

Jason smiled. "Let me think about it. We will talk to the palliative care group first and see what they have to say. Then I'll decide."

"No problems," Larissa replied with a smile. "I'll go and make you some breakfast. Do you have a specific request?"

"I'm craving yogurt, do we have any Dill?" Jason asked looking up at Dylan who was staring off out the window.

Dylan shook his head before nodding. "Um, yeah, yogurt, we have some strawberry yogurt I bought yesterday."

"Wonderful, how about some fruit to go with it?" Larissa asked.

Jason smiled and nodded his head. "That sounds terrific. Thank you."

Larissa left the room and Jason sighed. "Alright Dylan, out with it."

Dylan glanced down at his Papa and smiled. "I would really like it if you moved over to the Devil's compound. I'd feel more comfortable."

Jason smiled up at his son. "I will think about it. I want to make things easier on you son."

"Thank you, Papa."

I smiled over at my mate and stepped towards him. "I've got to go into work, but I promise I will be here tonight. Give me a ring if you need anything, anything at all. Larissa will be here all day, but if you just need a break or a chat, just give me a ring."

Dylan looked up at me and stood on tip toes to kiss my lips. "Thank you. For everything."

"My pleasure baby," I replied before turning to Jason who was doing his best to ignore us. "Have a relaxing day, Jason. I'll see you tonight."

"Have a good day at work, son. Try and stay out of trouble," he replied.

I chuckled and gave him a wave before I turned and left the house ready to head over to the AJE authority and start to find Ettore.

Chapter Eighteen

I entered the shifter unit room with a smile on my face and a pep in my step. There was nothing that could bring me down.

"Well, if it isn't the man of the moment," Coltrane said with a laugh as I rounded the corner.

My grin grew further, and I reached out and shook Coltrane's hand. "What can I say, the gods must love me."

Coltrane chuckled and patted me on the back. "You deserve it, man."

"So, what's on the agenda today?"

"We are just waiting on Kade to arrive and then we will be going through everything that Scout has been able to find out so far."

I nodded my head as Jasper walked up to me with a sly smile on his lips. He reached out and pulled the front of my shirt down to expose the mating mark. When he looked up at my face his smile grew.

I'm proud of you, he signed.

I opened my arms and he fell into my chest as I wrapped my arms around him in a tight bear hug, kissing the side of his head. I closed my eyes and sent out a silent prayer to the creator that they would one day find a mate for Jasper.

Where are you going to live now? Jasper signed when I let go of him.

On the compound. Dylan's Papa is dying, Larissa is talking him into moving over to the compound to die there so that Dylan and I can be together as well. His house is very small. He hasn't got much.

Jasper winced and shook his head. *I'm sorry about his Papa. Is there anything I can do?*

I shook my head and wrapped my arm around Jasper in another hug before signing to him, *just keep being you.*

"Thank you everyone for coming in," Kade said as he walked into the shifter unit room. We turned our attention to the big Nephilim as he strode to the front of the room with Scout by his side. "I'm going to turn this meeting over to Scout with all of the information that they've been able to find out."

Scout nodded their head and smiled. "First off, congratulations Jai," they said with a grin. I had no idea how they knew. "Right, so Ettore is holed up in the Morpheus training center. From our calculations, he has at least three hundred alphas in there with him and he is training them to fight. I was able to find out that there are rumors that he will be bringing in omegas to breed, but there has been no word on where he is planning on getting the omegas from or when."

"Where are these alphas from?" Israel asked. I could see the anger pouring off him. Landon, his mate was devastated by the loss of his sister. Israel wanted to destroy Ettore for that alone.

"Overseas. Unfortunately, while the AJE authority can work Australia-wide at shutting down breeding facilities, other countries aren't doing the same," Scout replied.

"How the hell did he get them into the country?" I asked.

"That's something we are trying to ascertain. It wasn't through any legal means, which tells me that he either has someone working for him that has the power to skip through space or he has got those powers."

Kade shook his head. "No. It must be someone working with him."

"What kind of supernatural can skip through space?" Memphis asked.

Arcadia stepped forward and smiled. "Demons."

"Alright, so now the goal is just to find out what demon he is working with," Memphis said.

Scout nodded their head. "They would be very powerful. Which means that they are possibly from the council."

"Rison hasn't said anything?" Kade asked.

"We hadn't thought about it being a demon that was helping him, but I will ask," Scout replied before unfocusing their eyes and moving their lips in a silent conversation. When they blinked their eyes back open, Scout frowned. "Rison said that they hadn't noticed any demons missing from the underworld, but he is going to do a more thorough check."

"Has he had any success in locating Lilith?" Hawke asked.

Scout nodded. "They know where she is residing but are only just able to go there now without being noticed. They had to wait for Ettore to be busy."

"What do we do in the meantime?" Oakland asked.

"We need a spy. Obviously, it can't be Lynx or Israel, as Ettore knows them," Arcadia said.

"Ettore knows pretty much everyone in the Devil's and Onyx Rebels," Hawke replied.

Scout hummed. "That's true."

"He doesn't know me," Alexander one of the human cops and Nash's brother-in-law said.

Kade nodded. "I'm not sure that it would work though with the fact that you are human. He is going to be instantly suspicious of any humans. We need a supernatural that he doesn't know."

"How young is the youngest alpha?" I asked.

"Thirteen," Scout replied.

"What about Justice? I asked Anghus. We could spin it that he wants to join the alphas, he heard about Ettore and wants to join in with them."

Anghus winced and shrugged his shoulders. "Maybe. Justice is strong, but I'm not sure if it would work."

"Harper, send Harper," Pax said. Harper was his mate's sister, who they had adopted. She was a strong alpha. One of the strongest I'd ever met aside from Anghus.

Anghus nodded his head. "She is strong enough. Are the other alphas male or female?"

"All male," Scout replied. "So, Harper might not be any good. But it is worth trying. If she wants to of course."

"Oh, she will want to, that girl has been after Ettore's blood since Rhyland was taken," Pax said with a growl in his voice.

"Alright, get her to come down so that we can speak to her. She will need to go through some training first, I don't want to send her in blind. She will need wards put over her mind so that Ettore can't read them," Kade said.

Pax nodded his head and pulled his phone from his pocket before stepping out of the room to ring his daughter. This could work. We could have the chance of bringing Ettore down from the inside out. I just hoped that Harper would be safe.

Chapter Nineteen

D ylan

It was such a good help that has Larissa helping with Papa. It gave me a chance to give the house a deep clean. Something I'd been wanting to do for months, but just didn't have time to do it. Papa had remained in bed for the whole day, which worried me, but I preferred him being in bed than walking around and potentially falling and hurting himself.

I was doing anything to keep my mind busy, because the minute I stopped, I started thinking about how I didn't have long left with my Papa. The truth was I wanted to curl up in the bed beside him and not leave his side. But I knew that wasn't practical.

When Harry came not long after ten to pick Flynn up, he'd come inside and hugged me and told me that he wasn't angry with me. I felt better knowing that I at least had my job. Not that I thought Jai would necessarily be alright with me dancing for anyone. Although he didn't have a problem fucking me in front of Flynn. He seemed to like it. I was a little confused, I wasn't complaining. It was the hottest thing I'd ever done.

By the afternoon the house was spotless, and Larissa had helped Papa to the couch, while we waited for the palliative care team to arrive. The door bell rang around two and when I answered the door two ladies stood on the other side wearing warm smiles.

"Hello, My name is Hilly, and this is Liza, we are from the palliative team to meet with Jason Ross."

I nodded my head. "Come on in, I'm Dylan, Jason's son."

"Nice to meet you, Dylan," Hilly replied as she stepped across the threshold. From the scent, I could tell that they were both supernatural shifters.

Once I led them into the living room, they took a seat on the couch opposite Papa. "It's nice to meet you, Jason and Larissa," Hilly started.

"Dr. Rankin contacted us last night to let us know about your case and to see what we could do to assist. He mentioned getting you a hospital bed, as well as some of the equipment that you will be requiring. Is there something that you specifically would like us to assist with?"

Papa shook his head. "To be perfectly honest, I'm not sure what I need."

Hilly smiled tenderly and nodded her head. "I understand. This time often comes as a bit of a shock to the family. Although they all know that you are sick, it's one of those things that still sneak up on us."

Papa nodded his head and sighed. "I am thinking that I might have to move from this house. There isn't a lot of room here."

Hilly glanced around our tiny living room. With the couch and two chairs in the space, it was already a tight squeeze. She nodded her head and smiled back at Papa. "Do you have somewhere that you can go? I can see that this is quite a small space, which can make things difficult for all the equipment you are going to require."

"Yes, I'm from the Devil's Advocates, we have homes available on our compound that Jason will be able to live in," Larissa answered.

Hilly's eyes lit up and she nodded her head. "Wonderful. Jason, what do you think about that?"

"I like the idea. I'm not attached to this place. It has always just been a place to live. My memories are all up in here," he said tapping on his head.

Hilly smiled and nodded. "I like that. Well, all we need to know is when you will be planning to move. We will deliver the equipment that is needed. We will stay in contact with you, should you need extra support. And Dylan, I'd like to offer you support too. Palliative care isn't just for the patient, it is for the family too."

"Thank you," I said as I cleared my throat.

Papa looked over at Larissa and smiled. "When would be suitable for the Devil's?" he asked.

"What if say the end of the week, that way palliative care can drop your equipment off and we can move you over there first. Then Dylan, Jai, and the other Devil can pack up the rest of the house to move over there, you don't need to be here for that. Unless you want to supervise?" Larissa answered.

Papa chuckled and shook his head. "No, no. Dylan is very capable. I know that he will be able to do it all."

Larissa smiled and turned back to Hilly and Liza. "Is that enough time for you?"

Hilly nodded her head. "Yes, that is fine. Larissa, what I'll do is grab some contact details for you, and we will ring you as soon as I get back to the office with a time of delivery, then we can go from there."

"Sounds perfect," Larissa said with a bright smile.

I looked over at Papa who was watching me. He gave me a wink. I felt for the first time some of the weight lift off my shoulders. It didn't take away from my grief, but it allowed me to know that Papa was going to be cared for. He didn't just have to rely on me anymore. He had a team of people willing to step in and help. It made me just like the Devil's Advocates that little bit more.

Chapter Twenty

J ai

"So, Jai is going to be the next to bring babies into the world," Anghus said with a smirk as we were kicked back in the shifter unit, waiting for Harper to arrive.

"Are we calling you Iver now?" I asked with a laugh.

Anghus chuckled and shook his head. "No, but I saw that knot was most definitely not wearing a condom the other night."

Lynx threw his head back and barked out a laugh, while Jasper chuckled beside me. "Dude. You were looking at my dick?" I said with wide eyes. "It's big, isn't it?"

Anghus rolled his eyes at me and laughed. "Not as big as mine or Bacchus's. When Bacchus knots inside me I feel it for a week."

"Ewww," I groaned making the guys laugh around me. "Never mention your ass and your mate's dick every again in my presence."

"At least you didn't have to see it. That image is going to be burned in my mind forever," Anghus cried.

I barked a laugh. "You could have slid the phone under the door."

"Right, and how was Dylan going to get it, you were literally stuck," Anghus argued making me laugh harder.

"I could've picked him up and carried him. I'm strong you know," I said as I lifted my arms to pump my muscles.

Anghus went to respond when Harper came bustling into the room and stopped placing her hands on her hips. "God, it smells like the alpha in here," she said with a crinkle of her nose.

"Harper girl," I cried before jumping from my seat and pulling her into my arms, pressing a kiss on her cheek.

"Ugh, get off me you big lug, don't you have a mate to annoy now?" she grizzled as she pushed me away and wiped at her cheek.

I grinned. "You love me," I said as I went and sat back down in the chair I'd vacated. Harper rolled her eyes and huffed a breath.

"Only cause Dad and Papa tell me I have to be nice to you," she replied, but the look on her face told me that there was not an ounce of dislike there. Harper was a hard little nut. On the inside, she was filled with gooey loveliness, but the shell, she wore on the outside was hard as steel.

"Okay guys, thanks to Harper for coming in, lets's get some planning," Kade said as he came into the room with Merza and Arcadia.

"What do you want me to do?" Harper asked.

"As you know Ettore is holed up at the Morpheus training center. We were hoping that maybe we can send someone in that will be able to feed us knowledge back. However, the problem is that Ettore knows all my AJE authority members and all the Devil's Advocates alphas and Onyx Rebels," Kade explained.

Harper nodded her head and folded her arms across my chest. "I've never met Ettore before, but is he likely to know me?"

Kade shook his head. "I don't believe so. He will know about Rhyland and what happened there, but what we are hoping is that we can come up with a story as to why you want to join in. He currently has three hundred alphas at the training center."

"Who are the alphas?" Harper said with a small frown on her face.

"I don't know. Rumors are running around, so I want to use those rumors to our advantage."

Harper nodded her head. "I can go there and say that I was pissed that Rhyland is back and getting all the attention. That Dad and Papa are turning him to be more human than supernatural. I'll tell him I want to join him because I heard that he wants to get rid of the humans."

Kade hummed and scratched at his chin. "That is a good story to go with. The only other problem we are facing is that all the alphas are men."

"So, do I fake being a boy?" Harper asked.

"Could you pull it off?" Pax asked, looking unconvinced.

Harper nodded her head. "Sure, I could. I could shave my head. Strap my boobs. He's not going to do a genital check is he?"

"No, I don't think he will," Arcadia said, but he is likely to read your memories.

"Can we put a ward over her to create false memories, similar to what we did with Rison?" Raiden asked.

Merza nodded her head. "I can do that. What will happen is that you have these memories that won't be a problem for you. But if someone tries to read you, those are the memories they will see. Your memories as being a girl, or being Harper, will be locked and the reader won't be able to see it."

Harper nodded. "Yeah, I'm happy with that. If I'm not going to forget who I am or anything like that."

Merza shook her head. "No, that won't happen, it will sort of be like giving you an extra personality, one you can draw on when you need it. However, it is going to take some time and training to complete it."

"How long have I got?" Harper asked, looking over at Kade.

"I'd like to send you in as soon as possible, but I won't be sending you until you are ready."

Harper nodded. "That doesn't really answer the question," she smarted, causing Kade to smirk. "But I can be ready. When would you like to start the training."

Merza smiled. "Why don't you come home with me, and we can start tonight. We will start by coming up with the personality that you want and then go from there. The wards will take about three days to complete. But then the training will take a few more days. I'd say in two weeks you will be ready to go."

"Sounds good to me," Harper said with a smile. "Hopefully I can see this cunt be brought down finally."

"You will be there to see it," Arcadia said. "It's just not going to happen yet."

Harper nodded her head. "I'm glad I get to see it."

Chapter Twenty-One

Dylan

By the end of the week, I'd managed to pack everything into boxes. Larissa told me that the palliative care group had been in constant contact, and they'd just delivered Papa's bed to the new house. Jai took me to have a look before we moved any furniture over, it was nice. There was loads of room for Papa's bed, and equipment that he would need, and the house was right next to the medical unit and across from the main house.

The Devil's compound was amazing. The main house sat in the center surrounded by forests, they had just about everything. Even a school. There were loads of kids about and everyone seemed to be happy. There were big houses that were for families, but they also had lots of small apartments that housed the single alphas and omegas.

At the very back of the property was a large garden, filled with vegetables and a fruit orchard, skirted along the border on two edges. They had chickens, and even cows, Jai explained that they were attempting to become completely self-sufficient. I loved the idea of it and couldn't wait to be able to get involved. This wasn't just a community; it was a family. They even all came together every Sunday to share a meal together that Larissa, Trudy, and Lucy made. Some of the omegas often helped with it too. Everyone had a role to play in the community.

"All set?" Papa asked as I taped up the last box.

I smiled and nodded my head. "Yeah, I'm leaving our beds here, Jai has organized for his bed to be moved over to the new house. If he had his way, he would have bought all new furniture," I replied with a chuckle.

Papa smiled. "I like that boy. He is perfectly suited to you. He has enough seriousness to appeal to that side of you, but enough joker in him to loosen you up a little."

I smiled and sat on the couch beside Papa, leaning over I rested my head on his shoulder. "I really like him too. Mother fate picked the perfect mate for me."

"She sure did. So, I hear the Devil's are our official movers tomorrow."

I nodded. "Yep. Larissa and Corson are coming to get you in the morning and then Anghus, Jai, his brother Jasper and a few of the others are coming with a truck to help move the rest of the stuff."

"Larissa has been a bit of a godsend."

"She sure has been. The whole MC has been such a huge help. Harry has been good too. He is paying me despite me not actually dancing that night."

"Hopefully now that you are mated, you won't have to work as much as you can take some time to relax and have fun."

I shrugged my shoulders. "I don't think I want to dance. But I like doing the waiting. That's always been fun."

Papa smiled and stroked his hand down over my hair. "I'm proud of you Dylan. I know that life wasn't easy for you once your Mama left. But I'm so damned proud of you."

I blinked my eyes to stop tears from falling and looked up at my Papa. "I love you, Papa. Even without Mama here, you made my life a fantastic one. I never needed anything. You always provided for me."

Papa sighed. "I tried my hardest. I feel so damned guilty that my body gave out on me before you had a chance to finish school."

"I have plenty of time to do that if I want to. It never bothered me to quit. You were and still are the most important thing in my life. I would never have kept going to school and left you to work it out. We are a team. Remember saying that to me when Mama left?"

Papa chuckled and nodded his head. "Yep. You were so angry at her. You wanted me to hunt her down and bring her home, but I couldn't do that. Not that I had any idea where she'd left to. But I knew that

I would do just about anything to make that smile come back to your face."

"I liked being your sidekick. I felt so grown up that day after our talk. It was the first time I ever saw you cry in front of me. You didn't hide any of your emotions, it made me feel like my anger was normal."

Papa smiled and took my hand in his, he lifted my hand and kissed my knuckles. "It was and is normal. You were most certainly allowed to feel that anger. Hell, I was angry, to be honest, I'm still pissed at her."

I sighed. "Yeah, me too," I replied with a shake of my head. I was furious. Not as angry as I had been. When I came home and found that note I was livid. I did want Papa to go and find her. I wanted her to be grown-up enough to tell me to my face that she didn't want me.

"Sometimes I wish I knew where she went just so I could go there and ask why?" I said with a sigh.

"I don't know that there was necessarily an answer. Well, probably not an answer that we would want to hear. Your Mama had a lot of inner demons, some that she didn't even realize she had. She grew up with a hard life. I think for your Mama I was just a way to escape her family and the situation she was thrust in. I was never meant to be her mate. We were never fated."

"That's the first time you've spoken about Mama's past."

Papa looked at me with surprise on his face. "Is it? Well, it wasn't a pretty life. She grew up with drug-addicted parents, who neglected her for the best part, at worst they paid attention to her. The attention was never good," Papa said with a sneer. "I met her when I was just out of high school. She was in the diner I was working at over the summer with her Papa, he slapped her across the face. I saw red and stepped in. From there we hung about a lot. My Papa had died the year before and my Mama was long gone, she died when she gave birth to me."

"Oh, I didn't know that" I replied. "Your life, was it good?"

"Yeah, up until my Papa died. It kind of resembled a little like us. The last year of my high school Papa got very sick with cancer, his was from a lifetime of smoking. He got lung cancer. He died just before I graduated. Anyway, after I met your Mama, we moved to Lalbert, I started working at the factory and your Mama worked for Lalbert Fire in the office taking emergency calls. We'd been together almost ten years when we finally had you. I was so excited the day she told me she was pregnant. I went to every check-up and test with her. Then when you came into the world, all red-faced and angry looking, I knew that being a Papa was the best job I could ever have."

I smiled. "I love you, Papa."

"I love you too, Dill."

Chapter Twenty-Two

J ai

I was so excited to move into the new house with Dylan and Jason. I'd stayed every night at Dylan's house and fucked him into the sheets most of the night. I really liked this mated gig.

"If you don't calm down, I'm going to have to chain you to the ground just to keep you from floating away," Anghus laughed as we walked up the front path towards Dylan's door.

I turned and grinned at my brother and widened my arms. "It's a beautiful day," I sang off-key and loud. "A wonderful day for love."

Anghus rolled his eyes but laughed and pushed me up the path. Dylan was standing at the door with his head cocked looking at me like I'd lost my mind. Maybe I had.

"Will you control your mate, he is like a kid with too much sugar," Anghus grumbled.

Dylan laughed and reached out grabbing my hand before leaning forward and planting a kiss on my lips. I moaned and licked at his bottom lip.

"Wanna sneak off into the bedroom, and let them do all the hard work?" I mumbled.

Dylan laughed as Anghus scoffed. "Come on you, there isn't a lot to move," he replied.

I followed Dylan and Anghus into the living room where Dylan had stacked all the boxes. I'd managed to talk him into leaving all the big furniture behind in favor of new furniture. Jason owned the house that they lived in, and I'd suggest maybe renting it out to make a bit of a wage for them. Jason was all for the idea. Dylan wasn't sure that they'd be able to rent in the condition it was in. But with a promise that the Devil's would come and fix anything that needed fixing, he said he thought it was a good idea.

It didn't take long for us to stack the boxes into the back of the truck with plenty of room to spare. Anghus, Lynx, and Arley were making sure nothing would move as Dylan and I stood in the living room.

"This is the only house I've ever lived in," he said quietly.

"It won't be gone, you still have it," I reminded him.

Dylan looked over at me and smiled, nodding his head. "I guess it just feels weird. It will be nice to live in a bigger house. But it feels strange to be living somewhere else. It will feel even stranger when Papa is gone."

I reached out my arms and pulled him into my chest, kissing the top of his head. "I will be with you, and we will walk the journey together."

"Thank you," Dylan whispered as I rubbed my hands up and down his back.

"Hey, did I miss all the moving?" Flynn called from the front door. "Oh, what a pity, I was going to help."

Dylan looked up at me and rolled his eyes. "How were you going to help with your leg still in a cast?"

I turned to see Flynn hobbling his way into the living room. "I could've done something," he laughed, "I could've supervised."

Dylan chuckled and went to his friend, pressing a kiss to his cheek. "How did you get here?"

"Harry drove me, he is out there talking to Anghus."

"Did you see that Arley is here too?" I teased.

Flynn's eyes widened and his cheeks tinted pink. "Is he?"

I barked out a laugh. "How can you be so coy around Arley when you were happy to watch me fuck my mate?"

Flynn shrugged his shoulders. "I don't know. Maybe it's caused Dylan's my best friend. I don't know."

"Is there any more to go out to the truck?" Arley said as he came in through the front door.

I chuckled and shook my head. "Arley, meet Flynn, Dylan's best friend."

Flynn's face bloomed red, the reddest I'd ever seen the man blush. Arley pushed his sunglasses to the top of his head and pulled the hood from his head.

"Hey Flynn," the vampire said with a smirk, that read he knew exactly who Flynn was. I may or may not have told him.

"Um, hi, nice to meet you," Flynn said as he ducked his head.

"Flynn are you flirting with Arley?" Harry said as he came in through the door.

"Oh, for god's sake," Flynn muttered causing us all to laugh.

Harry pressed a kiss to the top of Flynn's head. "I was just talking to Arley outside and said he should come and have dinner with us one night."

Flynn's eyes flung open, and he looked up at Harry. Dylan chuckled and leaned into my side.

"Would that be alright, little unicorn?" Arley said crowding into Flynn.

Flynn bit into his bottom lip and nodded his head. Arley's grin turned predator as he took in Flynn. Oh, boy to be a fly on the wall that night.

Chapter Twenty-Three

Dylan

Papa was already set up in the house. We'd made the living room into a makeshift bedroom. He looked exhausted just from the move. Dr. Rankin came out to visit and make sure we had everything we needed, along with the palliative care ladies, Hilly and Liza. Larissa had done a great job setting everything up. She connected Papa up to a drip with a button that he could push to give him a dose of morphine.

Papa didn't complain much but I saw the relief on his face as the morphine started to do the job. I never realized how much pain he was in until he was able to get the relief. It made me feel guilty that I never knew how much pain he was in. A lot of the children came to visit and introduce themselves.

I met Anghus's son Iver. He was a hoot. I didn't know much about other supernaturals, but Iver was out of this world. He explained to me that he was able to converse with the creator. I was in awe. I wanted to sit and talk to him for hours to hear everything. I made sure not to ask anything that I might not want the answer to, but I could see that Iver knew.

"That's the last box," Jai said as he folded the last box after packing away the last of the kitchen supplies.

"It didn't take very long at all," I replied.

Jai grinned and lifted his arms to flex his muscles. "It's because I'm superman, baby."

I laughed and shook my head. I reached out my hand and squeezed his hard bicep and moaned. "Superman just happens to be my favorite superhero."

Jai flashed me a bright grin and leaned forward pressing a kiss to my lips. "I'm going to enjoy fucking you tonight in our new room."

I moaned and stepped into his arms. Jai wrapped his arms around my back and squeezed my ass. My cock swelled and when I pressed my hips against Jai's I could feel that he was hard too.

"Hey Dylan," Larissa called as she came into the kitchen. "Shit, sorry."

I broke the kiss with a laugh. "Sorry, we shouldn't be making out in the kitchen. What can I do for you?"

Larissa chuckled. "I should be used to seeing it. I've walked in on Jasper way too many times to count."

Jai barked out a laugh. "The problem with him being deaf, he can't hear when we knock. I've seen way more of him than I think is reasonable."

I giggled. "Well, we gave Anghus a sight to see."

Jai threw his head back and laugh. "He still hasn't got over that."

Larissa shook her head. "Anyway, I've got to pop out to the medical unit, I've got a pregnant omega that is being brought in, she managed to escape a breeding facility."

"Oh, that's fine, I'll be here with Papa. Is there anything he needs now?"

Larissa shook her head. "No, he's had his dose of medications and is sleeping, I just wanted to let you know before I left so that you didn't wonder where I was."

"That's fine. Thanks, Larissa, for everything. You've been amazing."

Larissa winked at me. "Anytime sweetheart, I love what I do."

I smiled and watched as the vampire turned and left the kitchen. "I'm going to go and take a quick shower, I think I stink," Jai said.

"Okay, I'll make us some lunch while you're in the shower and then I'll see if Papa is hungry for some soup."

Jai leaned forward and pressed a kiss on my lips. "Thanks, baby. Oh, and Iver said, to take a pregnancy test. I forgot to tell you."

My eyes widened. "He knows, doesn't he?"

Jai laughed and nodded his head. "Yep. He struggles to hold anything back when the creator tells him. He is working on it, but sometimes it just blurts out of him."

"Did he tell you whether I was pregnant?"

Jai's eyes sparkled as he nodded his head. "Yep."

"And?"

Jai threw his head back and laughed before kissing the end of my nose. "And go and do a pregnancy test," he replied with a wink.

I rolled my eyes but grinned. "I will after lunch. But give me a hint, does he know what we are having?"

Jai laughed again before making a zipper action across his lips and pretending to throw away a key.

"Oh, come on," I whined.

"I can't hear you," Jai sang as he turned from the kitchen and headed for our bedroom and bathroom.

That bloody tease.

Chapter Twenty-Four

Jai Dylan out of the bathroom with a smile that could only be described as radiant. He held up the pregnancy test and giggled.

I laid back on the bed. "Wait," I said rubbing my temples. "Let me use my psychic powers. I believe that it is going to say that you are most definitely pregnant."

Dylan laughed again and rolled his eyes. "It does indeed. Wanna come into the living room so that I can tell Papa?"

I nodded my head and stood from the bed. "First," I said as I pulled him into my arms, "I need to kiss the Papa."

Dylan moaned and opened his lips for me to sweep my tongue over his. I thrust my hands up into his hair and tilted his head so that I could deepen the kiss. I broke the kiss before we got too carried away. There was plenty of time for love. First, I wanted to give Jason some good news.

We went into the living room that was converted into a bedroom for Jason. His bed sat in the center of the room with equipment all around him. An I.V tube stuck into his arm. His skin was grey, and I noticed that his lips were a darker color than normal. Almost like they were bruised. His eyes were half-closed.

Dylan stopped at the edge of the bed, and I felt the fear start to pour from him. "Papa?" he said with a hitch in his voice. "Papa?" Dylan started to sound more panicked. Suddenly he dropped the pregnancy test and ran to the head of the bed. "No Papa, not now. Papa, I have good news for you. Wake up, please Papa." Tears trekked down Dylan's cheeks as he cried for his Papa to open his eyes. But it was too late. He was gone.

It had happened so quickly. I'd had a shower while Dylan made us lunch. We sat with Jason while he tried to swallow down some soup. He'd been having trouble swallowing. Dylan was patient as he slowly brought it to his father's lips. Jason had told Dylan he loved him and thanked him for a wonderful lunch. He told us that he wanted to sleep for a little while, so I cleaned the kitchen while Dylan was in the bathroom.

He wasn't in there longer than twenty minutes. I hadn't stopped to check on Jason before I went into the bedroom to wait for Dylan to return with the pregnancy test. I figured he would be alright.

"I'll go and find Larissa," I said, unsure what else I could do. As I turned to leave the front door opened and Larissa came rushing in.

"Iver came and found me," she said as she went over to Jason. She placed two fingers on his wrist, before moving her fingers to his neck. She shook her head at me and sighed. "I'm sorry Dylan. I'm so sorry."

Dylan didn't say anything, but his sobs sounded through the whole room. We all knew that it was going to happen, but nothing had truly prepared me for that moment. I walked over to Dylan and wrapped my arms around my mate. He stood from his Papa's body and fell into my arms.

"Why now? He was fine at lunch, why did the creator choose now. I was just going to tell him about the baby," Dylan cried.

"He knows baby, he knows," I said.

"How?" Dylan asked.

"Iver told him when we first moved him over here. Jason said he had a dream that a little boy called Iver had a message for him. We'd all be shocked as anything, but Anghus went and got Iver straight away. Iver told him about the baby," I explained.

Dylan sighed. "Was he happy?"

"Ecstatic. He told me that I was to look after you while you were pregnant or he would come and haunt me every time I was about to cum," I said with a chuckle as I remembered the conversation.

"Oh, my gods," Dylan groaned. "That is so my father."

I laughed again. "He was an amazing man, and I've been so blessed to have known him, even though it was only a short time. I'm beyond grateful to Mother fate for bringing you into my life."

Dylan looked up at me with watery eyes. "I love you, Jai."

I smiled and pressed a small kiss to Dylan's nose. "I love you too, Dylan."

"What do we do now?" Dylan asked glancing back over to Larissa who was preparing a bowl and a wash cloth to prep Jason's body.

"Jason asked me to give you this when the time came," Larissa said as she lifted an envelope from the drawer that was beside the bed.

Dylan frowned and took the envelope from Larissa. He slid his finger underneath the flap and took out the letter. Tears started to flood Dylan's cheeks as he looked down at the paper. He shook his head and handed me the letter.

"I can't, can you read it please?" he asked.

"Of course, baby," I replied as I took the letter from Dylan. "To my amazing son. I love you with all my heart. Words can't express just how proud I am to have had eighteen wonderful years being your Papa. I have always been proud of you. Every milestone, every achievement, and every choice has filled me with pride. I know that you too are going to be the most wonderful Papa. I'm sorry that I won't be around to meet my grandchildren, but I will be watching. I will be sitting beside you, guiding your every step."

Dylan let out a little sob, but my heart was so full of love. The pride and love that Jason had for his son, seemed to seep through the page of the letter.

"I have organized my funeral. You will find the paperwork in my file. I am to be cremated and then I want you to sprinkle me in the ocean. I never got to spend very much time-shifted and, in the ocean, as I would have liked to. So, I also urge you to make a difference. Make sure you take your babes and teach them all the things that I wish I'd done with you."

Dylan smiled and nodded his head. "I'll do that," he promised.

"Dylan, I don't know if you want to know or not, but I have included in this letter where you can find your mother. She got in contact with me when you were fifteen, but you were still so angry with her that I never told you. I don't know if I was right or wrong in that choice. However, if you want closure, I've included her contact details. I love you son. Keep being the best man that I know you are. Love with all your heart, enjoy every day, kiss, make love often, and be happy. Love Papa."

I folded the paper over and saw the address and name of Dr. Lilibeth Carlisle. I assumed that she was Dylan's mother. Her name was familiar, but I didn't know where I knew it from. I figured it would come to me eventually.

"I don't want to see that bitch," Dylan spat.

"You don't have to baby," I said with a smile. No matter what he chose I would be by his side.

Chapter Twenty-Five

Dylan

Everything seemed to move so fast, but so slow at the same time. Anghus came with Dr. Rankin who organized for Papa's body to be moved over to the crematorium. Then it was a matter of going through paperwork and shutting down accounts, finalizing payments on his medical bills, and having the deed of the house changed over into my name. I felt sick. I didn't know that I would have coped at all if it hadn't been for having Jai and the rest of the Devil by my side.

Harry and Flynn helped as much as they could, but they had their own lives and things to do. Flynn and Arley had been spending more time together and I wished I had the energy to know what was going on there. I was curious but just didn't have the energy to do more than sit and cry. Papa had only spent one night at the new house. That was it.

Dr. Rankin tried to explain that sometimes when it comes to an end, it comes as a shock to the family. The patient tends to decide that it's time. They stop fighting. I guess that was what it was for Papa. He knew that I had someone. He knew that my life was about to become busier with a new baby in the mix and although I wished he had stayed long enough to see the baby born, I knew that he was happy to go before then. I could just imagine how much harder things would have been to have a baby and a sick Papa at the same time.

Not that the thought made losing him any easier. It hurt, it hurt like hell. I'd read and re-read his letter over and over. I always stopped short of him telling me about my Mama. I appreciated that Papa hadn't told me when she turned back up. I know that a lot of people would have been mad at Papa for keeping that to himself. But it just showed to me how much Papa truly knew me. He knew that there was no possible way I would want anything to do with that horrid woman.

I decided against having a big funeral for Papa. He didn't have any family left, and his friends had drifted away when he got sick. Instead, the Devil's held a special dinner in honor of my Papa. Anghus told me that they would like to celebrate the next Devil to be born, I liked the sound of that. I knew that my Papa wouldn't want me missing out on my pregnancy by mourning. But every time I thought about it, I would poke my tongue out at the sky in spite. I wanted to cry. But I also knew that it was coming time to dry the tears and start living again.

He'd been gone for just over two weeks when we had our very first ultrasound appointment. I was going to get to see my baby for the first time. I'd received Papa's ashes in a box and took them with me. I made a promise that I was going to take them to the ocean and let them drift on the waters, it was something I wanted to do, but first I wanted him to be with me when we saw the baby.

I'd planned with Jai for us to go out to the ocean after the appointment and do the releasing then. I wanted to swim with the ashes while shifted and have that final goodbye to my Papa. Jai thought it was a wonderful idea. He said it had been quite a while since he'd shifted just for fun. Although his chimera wasn't one to swim, he would fly over the top of me.

I was excited, nervous, grief-stricken, happy, and sad all rolled into one. I couldn't really describe the feeling that I had, but it was a bundle of confusion. I wanted to bounce in the seat and be as excitable as Jai was, but at the same time, it was so bittersweet. My Papa's ashes sat heavy in my lap as we waited for my name to be called.

"Dylan?" a lady with bright pink hair called. I smiled and stood as Jai practically bounced out of the seat beside me. "And you must be Jai."

"I am," he said with a smile as he took my hand and led me towards the lady.

"It's nice to meet you both, although, I think I've met you before Jai. I'm Reagan, I'm the radiologist here."

"It's lovely to meet you too," I replied as she led us into a small, darkened room with a bed in the center.

"Alright, if you want to lie up on your back on the bed for me and just lift your shirt, we can get started," Reagan instructed.

I nodded my head and placed Papa's ashes in the seat beside Jai before lying on the bed and lifting my shirt. My belly hadn't protruded much, but it was starting to develop a small little round pudge there. I loved it and I couldn't' wait to be huge and pregnant, feeling our baby kick and wriggle.

"Alright just some gel," Reagan said as she squirted the blue gel onto my belly before pressing a wand down. "Beautiful. Baby is looking very healthy."

"Just one?" Jai asked.

"Yep, just a single baby, were you hoping for more?"

"I didn't mind, but I do want loads of kids one day," Jai replied with a smile. I would keep giving him kids forever if it meant I got to see that beautiful smile on his face.

"Well, everything is looking good, measurements are all correct and baby looks like they are doing very well. I can even tell you what you are having if you'd like to know?" Reagan asked.

I nodded my head. "I think Jai already knows, but he won't tell me."

Reagan chuckled. "Yes, I've been hearing about this little detector you've got out there at the Devil's compound."

Jai laughed and nodded. "He is something spectacular. Let's see if he got this one right too."

I looked back over at Reagan who smiled down at me. "How about at the count of three Jai and I say it at the same time?"

I laughed and nodded my head. "Alright. One, Two, Three."

"Boy," they both said simultaneously.

"Iver got it right again," Jai laughed.

"A boy. Oh, my stars," I said with a smile.

Jai pressed a kiss to the top of my head. "Our little boy, Jason," Jai said quietly.

I gasped and looked up at my mate. "Really? You would want to name him Jason?"

"With all my being. Plus, the creator told Iver that's what his name was."

I chuckled. "I love it."

"Me too," Jai said as he pressed another kiss to my cheek.

Chapter Twenty-Six

J ai

"Thank you for coming in at short notice," Kade said as he came into the shifter room. The night before he'd sent a message through Anghus that he wanted to meet with all the inner Devil's, Harper, the shifter unit, and Onyx Rebels. That meant that there had been a development in the case with Ettore.

Harper had been training full on with Merza, Arcadia, Scout, and Oakland. We were expecting that she would be sent in any day. It had been two weeks since we released Jason's ashes to the ocean. It was such a beautiful yet sad moment. Dylan had shifted into a kelpie and swam out with his father's ashes while I flew overhead.

What none of us had expected was the large pod of dolphins that surrounded the ashes and seemed to guide them out to the middle of the ocean. It was the most awe-inspiring sight.

"Did you see that?" Dylan had cried through the link.

"Yeah baby, they are taking your Papa home," I said as I sniffed back tears.

That night we'd stayed in and just rested on the couch. It felt weird not having Jason around anymore and every day that passed it got a little easier. But that hole was still there.

I tuned my attention back to Kade who had taken his place at the front of the shifter unit room. "I got word from Rison late last night. Ettore has called him back to earth. Apparently, he wants Rison to train with the alphas."

"This can work in our favor for sure," Arley said. "With Harper going in, then we've got someone to watch out for her, but with the two of them working together, it will work even better."

Kade nodded his head. "Exactly what I was thinking."

"So, when is Rison coming?" I asked.

"Today. He should be at the training center already. I would like to give it one more week before we send Harper in. I don't want it to be too soon between Rison coming back and us sending Harper. The last thing we want is Ettore to clue that Rison is working against him."

"I agree," Merza replied. "Harper is almost ready. In fact, she is probably at a point where she could go on any day. There are just a couple of things I'd like to get done for sure."

"Do we have her story sorted out?" Memphis asked.

Merza nodded her head. "We do."

I turned to the door as a bald Harper strutted into the room. If it wasn't for the fact that I knew this was Harper, I'd be convinced she was just a small guy. Harper was a meerkat shifter, so she was small anyway. But so was Holland.

"Meet, Ryder Fitzgibbon," Merza said with a wave of her hand.

Before my very eyes, Harper morphed, like nothing I'd ever seen before. No longer was the tough little girl standing in front of us, but she seemed to grow, her face even appeared to alter. Yet it didn't at the same time.

"Did anyone else see that?" I asked.

Merza chuckled. "Basically, the way that we have worked this spell, Harper and Ryder are two different people. It's a bit like when someone has DID or what used to be called multiple personality disorder. Instead of it happening through trauma, instead, we have created it. Harper is still there, and she can consciously switch between the two personalities. However, Ryder is his own person."

"Holy shit," I whispered.

"What happens once Ettore is dead though?" Coltrane asked.

Merza winced. "Unfortunately, it will be impossible for us to get rid of Ryder. He will always be a part of Harper. She was made fully aware of this before we put the spell on her and understands. Every day that Ryder lives the more real he becomes. That's why we wanted to take our time before sending him in."

"Is there are chance that Ryder will take over Harper?" Arley questioned.

Merza shook her head. "No. There is a split so that only Harper can control which personality is at the front. Ryder doesn't have the choice to step forward unconsciously. Harper must make the switch."

I nodded my head. I didn't know a lot about science or what went on with witches and warlock spells, but it was so interesting to see Ryder stand in front of us.

"So, what is your story, Ryder?" Kade asked.

Ryder looked over at Kade and gave a lop-sided smile. "I'm eighteen years old. Born in Philadelphia, USA," he said with the perfect American accent. My mouth dropped open. This was the most amazing thing I'd ever witnessed.

Kade grinned and looked over at his mate. "You've done a great job babe," he said with a smirk.

Merza winked at him and gave him a smile. There was no way that Ettore could win against us.

Chapter Twenty-Seven

D ylan
I yawned and stretched in bed. My hips and lower back were aching with carrying around a baby all day. I was almost at the finish point and as much as I loved being pregnant, I was well and truly ready for this part of the journey to be over. I wanted to meet our little man, Jason.

We'd painted his nursery in deep blues and greens. It was funny to watch Jai get so excited over the littlest things. The other day we discovered a tiny set of booties and Jai gushed over them for an hour.

"You alright baby," Jai asked as he rubbed his hand up my back.

I moaned and rolled more onto my side. "I will be fantastic if you keep rubbing my back like that," I mumbled into my pillow.

Jai chuckled and continued to massage my back, down my hips, and over my thighs. I let out a long moan as I felt the muscles soften under his hands.

"You keep moaning like that and you are going to wake up little Jai," he said with a laugh.

I giggled and wriggled my hips back against him. "Is that so?"

Jai moaned and stroked his hand down over my bare ass and ran his fingers through the crease. "That is so. Do you want to wake him?"

"I think I do," I moaned as Jai circled my hole with the tip of his finger before pushing it inside me.

"You're wet and ready," he whispered in a husky voice.

"I'm always wet and ready for you," I laughed.

Jai moved his hand and roved around to the front of me, circling his palm around my shaft that was hard and throbbing. "You certainly are."

I moaned in delight as he continued to move his hand up and down my shaft, rolling his palm over the weeping head and back down again to my balls.

"Roll on your back baby, I want to taste you," Jai purred.

I rolled to my back and watched through hooded lids as Jai flipped the blankets back and moved down the bed. I could just see the top of his head over my belly as he licked the top of my dick. I groaned and thrust my hips. Jai swallowed me down his throat and my eyes rolled to the back of my head, causing my toes to curl. I grasped hold of the sheets below me to anchor me to the ground.

Jai continued his onslaught, of sucking, licking, and kisses up and down my shaft, before moving to my balls and sucking each one into his mouth. I was groaning and making all sorts of noises. I was never going to get enough of this man. Even when we were old men with walking sticks, I could see that Jai and I would still be like horny teenagers.

He kissed up along my thighs and over my belly. "I want you to ride me, baby."

I smiled and climbed to my knees as Jai lay on his back. Turning so that my back was facing him I straddled Jai's legs. Jai reached out and clasped my ass cheeks in his hands as I reached between my legs and slid his cock over my hole. Slowly I lowered my hips and felt his cock breech my hole. With a gasp, my eyes rolled, and I rocked back and forth on my mate.

"Fuck baby, you feel so fucking good," Jai moaned as I continued to rock back and forth.

"I want you to knot me. I want it to be the biggest knot you've ever given me. I want to be so fucking full of you," I moaned as every roll of my hips caused Jai's cock to stroke over my prostate.

"Oh, fuck yes," Jai moaned. I stroked my hands up and down Jai's thighs and curled my fingers to lightly scratch over his balls. "Fuck, just like that baby."

I could feel Jai's knot beginning to form as I continued to rock. My balls were tight, and my orgasm was right on the edge. "Give me that big knot Jai. I need it. I want to cum so hard," I moaned.

Jai's breathing was choppy, and I could feel that he was close. "I'm cumming baby, fuck I'm cumming."

Jai's knot locked into place, and it was exactly what I needed. I roared as jets of warm cum sprayed down over Jai's legs and the sheets below. Jai ran his hands up and down my back, pressing into the sore muscles as I leaned forward and rested my weight onto his legs.

"I love you so fucking much, Dylan," Jai said, breaking the silence of the room.

A lazy smile formed on my lips, and I glanced at him over my shoulder. "I love you too, Jai."

Chapter Twenty-Eight

J ai

"Are you sure you're ready to do this?" I asked Harper as we sat in the shifter room unit.

She smiled up at me and nodded her head. "I am. Ryder is. We've got this."

I shook my head. "I don't think I'm ever going to get used to seeing Ryder."

Harper laughed. "It took me a little while to get used to having a second person in my brain, but I like him, she said with a blush."

"Can you see him? Like what he looks like? That sort of thing?"

Harper nodded her head. "Yeah, it's weird. It's like being in a room and when we are in there together of a night when I'm sleeping, I can see him, touch him, and smell him just like I can you now."

My eyes widened and I gasped. "So, he is like a real living, breathing person, just inside your head."

"Yep. It is weird huh?"

"What's he look like?"

"He has dark brown, long hair that is curly like I'm talking mass of curls. His skin is tanned like he spends ages in the sun. His eyes are almost golden."

"And did you develop what he looked like or that just what he appeared to you?" My curiosity was piqued. I couldn't imagine what it would be like to suddenly have a whole new person living inside me.

"No, I fell asleep while Merza and Oakland did the spell and while I was asleep, I was in this room that is like a living room. The door opened and Ryder walked in."

"No shit? That is amazing."

Harper laughed and nodded her head. "Yeah, that's what I thought too. At first, I was a little nervous. What if we hated one another or he wanted to take over. But we just seemed to fit. I don't know if the spell worked that way, that our personalities would fit so perfectly or if it is just who Ryder is."

"Could it be like a mate?" I asked.

Harper hummed and shrugged her shoulders. "Maybe. But I don't know. Like he doesn't smell like a mate. He smells just like me, I guess. I don't know. It's hard to explain, but it's like he is just me, and I'm him."

"Yeah, I don't get," I said with a laugh and shake of my head. "But I'm glad you've worked it out. I'm still going to worry about you going in."

Harper sighed. "I'm ready. I was frustrated because it was taking so much longer than we were anticipating but I understood why we had to hold back."

"Yeah, Ettore doesn't trust anyone, so we had to make sure that Rison was well and truly embedded before risking sending you in. The last thing I want is anything to happen to you. I know that Pax and Holland would tear the place apart if something did happen."

Harper smiled and nodded her head. "I will be fine. Ryder has me well protected. Ettore won't know that I'm even there."

"Good," I said as I slung my arm around her shoulder and kissed the top of her bald head.

"Alright, Harper and Ryder are you ready to go in?" Kade asked as he came into the room.

Harper looked up at him and smiled before she sunk to the back and Ryder took her place. It always took me by surprise the sheer difference that happened when Ryder stepped forward. Harper's body language and face changed. Her jaw set firm, her shoulders raised up and I swear she even became bulkier.

"I'm ready," Ryder replied.

Kade smiled and nodded his head. "Israel is going to be watching you from the wall. You know the story?"

"Yep, I heard the rumors that Ettore wants to end humans. I want to join in."

"Good. At any moment that there seems to be trouble, I want you to press the panic button. We will get you out of there," Kade said.

I didn't know how they planned to get Harper and Ryder out if there was trouble, but I had to trust that Kade had it all planned.

"We've got this," Ryder said with another firm head nod before turning to face me. He stuck his hand out for me to shake. "I'll look after her."

I smiled and nodded my head. "Good."

Ryder then stepped back so that Harper could step forward. She went to each person in the room and wrapped her arms around them, hugging them tightly. Pax and Holland both had tears in their eyes. Aurora sobbed into her mate's chest. Walker's face was set firm, but I could see the fear in his eyes. None of us knew exactly what was about to happen, but all we could do was pray for the best.

I'd asked Iver if he had any insight, but all he could say was that Harper would be well protected. I didn't know if that meant Harper and Ryder would be successful in this plan, but I just hoped that the girl would come out the other side relatively unscathed.

Chapter Twenty-Nine

Dylan

"Okay baby, it's time to come out into the world," I said down to my belly. I was three days overdue and from all looks of things, Jason was in no hurry to come into the world.

Everyone was on tenterhooks waiting for his arrival, but there seemed to be no sign of him showing up anytime soon. I'd tried everything. I'd gone for a ride on the back of Jai's bike, over bumpy roads, we'd had sex, I drank raspberry leaf tea, which is disgusting by the way. I even took a dose of castor oil, which only made me gag.

"Still no signs of the wee man?" Lynx asked as I waddled my way down to the garden, in hope that some weeding might encourage him to come on out.

I shook my head and sighed. "He is obviously very comfortable."

Lynx chuckled and nodded his head. "It sure seems that way. He will come when he is ready."

I smiled and nodded before continuing onto the garden. The vegetable garden was huge, and I loved being there. I'd got to know a few of the others that worked in the garden, Trudy a siren, who was absolutely drop-dead gorgeous. She would give models a run for their money, Lucy who often worked in the kitchen, and Landon, Israel's mate. He was slowly starting to overcome the death of his sister, Brooklyn. But sometimes I still saw him staring off into the distance, towards the cemetery that was connected to the compound.

My heart ached for him. I knew what it was like to lose someone. I still thought about Papa every day. And some days I couldn't stop the tears from flowing. I knew that he was still around watching. There would be times that I would see him reflected in a bird's eyes or experience that I had.

Trudy was kneeling in amongst the garden beds, plucking the weeds that had popped their heads up around the zucchini.

"Morning Dylan how are you feeling this morning?" she called with a cheery smile.

"I'm doing good thank you. Just wishing my son would come into the world already," I replied with a laugh.

Trudy chuckled and nodded. "I have never been pregnant, but I'm not the most patient person in the world, so I can imagine how frustrating it would be."

"Yeah, it's getting a little tiresome. I just want to meet him already," I replied as I kneeled beside Trudy and started to pull weeds.

"So, you are all set up?" she asked.

"Yes, Jai has been like a scout. He has got everything. I'm not sure that we will need clothes until Jason is at least four. He has just about every contraption there is."

Trudy barked out a laugh. "Every time I speak to him, he raves about some latest gadget that he found that will help raise Jason better."

I rolled my eyes and laughed. "Yep, we have bought everything on the market."

Harry and Flynn had come around and laughed when they saw just how much stuff we had. There was no way that we were even going to use half of what we had. But I couldn't say no to Jai. He was so excited. I'd heard the horror stories that many omegas are told that alphas will mate with you and then leave you to raise the children. But that wasn't how it was with Jai. He loved being a part of this baby's life. Hell, if Jai had his way, I'd be popping out babies left-right, and center.

I bent forward to pull a weed out on the other side of the garden bed when I felt a pop, suddenly a gush of fluid splashed and soaked the ground beneath me. My eyes widened and I gasped.

"What is it?" Trudy asked. "Did you hurt yourself?"

I shook my head. "No. But my water just broke."

"Oh my god. Are you okay? Should I get someone?"

I shook my head again as I stood slowly and glanced between my legs at the large puddle at my feet. "No, I'm alright, I'm not having any contractions yet. I'll head up to the medical unit though."

"Alright, I'll come with you," Trudy said as she stood and dusted her hands off on her jeans.

I pulled my phone out and pressed on Jai's number before bringing it to my ear.

"Hey baby," Jai answered.

"Hi there. My water just broke. I'm in the garden and I'm heading up to the medical bay now," I explained.

"Oh my god, we're gonna have a baby," Jai crowed. "I'll be at the medical bay in a moment."

I nodded my head and said goodbye before ending the call and walking up the medical bay. There were still no contractions, but it was uncomfortable walking when every step squirted more water out and down my leg.

By the time Trudy and I reached the medical bay, Larissa was already standing out the front with Jai who was bouncing on his toes. His excitement was pouring off him. He turned and looked at me with a bright smile. My stomach had started to cramp slightly, but there was still nothing major.

"How are you doing Dylan?" Larissa asked.

"Fine now. I'm having some minor cramps. Nothing painful," I answered.

"Alright, well I've rang Dr. Rankin, he said that you are right to head into the hospital whenever you feel necessary. If you aren't in any pain now, I'd suggest going and having a warm shower and just trying to relax until the contractions start to ramp up. Then head in," Larissa explained.

I nodded my head. "Yeah, that sounds like a good plan," I replied as I left Larissa and Trudy. Jai took me into the bathroom and helped me to step out of my soaked pants, before flipping the taps on the shower and getting it to a good temperature.

"Are you doing alright baby?" he asked.

"Yeah, for now, I don't imagine it's going to stay this easy though," I said with a laugh.

J ai

"Fucking get this big-headed fucking kid out of me," Dylan roared as he bore down through another contraction. He had my hand in a firm death grip. His hair stuck to his head with sweat and his face was red with exertion.

"Almost there Dylan, I can see the top of his head. One more push and you will have his head out," Dr. Rankin said calmly from his position between Dylan's legs.

I felt about as useless as a turd on a stick. I wanted to take the pain away from my mate. I wanted to reach in and pull the baby out for him. There was just nothing I could do. I had to let him do all the hard work and just hold his hand through it.

We'd been at home for about six hours before the contractions had begun to get more comfortable than he could bear. By the time we reached the hospital, Dylan was swearing and doubled over in pain. We'd only been in the hospital room for about thirty minutes when he said that he needed to push.

Nurses and Dr. Rankin were running around, getting everything ready, while I stood by like a lump watching my mate go through the most excruciating pain of his life.

"Jesus, why does he have such a big fucking head," Dylan growled through grit teeth as he bore down again.

Dr. Rankin chuckled. "We've got the head out. Good job. Halfway there. Just hold off for a second so I can check the cord."

Dylan breathed out a heavy sigh and closed his eyes. "You are doing so good baby, I'm so fucking proud of you."

Dylan glanced up at me a smiled. "I'm happy that you're proud of me, but just don't put another baby in me for a long while."

I barked out a laugh and nodded my head. "Alright, I'll wait a few months."

Dylan's eyes narrowed but before he could say anything he gasped. "Oh, can I push, I need to push," he said frantically.

"Yep, push this baby on out," Dr. Rankin replied.

With one large push, I watched as our son shot into the world into the doctor's arms. His dark hair was stuck to his head and his face was red and angry. He let out a loud booming roar that I swore echoed the delivery room.

"Well, he's certainly got some lungs on him," Dr. Rankin chuckled. "Meet your son."

Dr. Rankin laid Jason on Dylan's chest. Dylan looked down at our son with a warm smile. "Hey there baby Jason."

Jason stopped his cry long enough to look up into his Papa's eyes. "He's beautiful. So beautiful," I said as tears blurred my eyes.

"Dad, wanna come and cut the cord?" Dr. Rankin asked.

I nodded my head with a grin as I took the scissors from the doctor's hands. I cut through the cord where he pointed to before looking back up at my mate and son as they bonded. I couldn't have asked for a more perfect moment.

Epilogue

Jai

I loved having my son home. I couldn't get enough of him. His smell, the feel of his warm body. I was the first to leap out of bed when he cried. It didn't matter what he needed I was happy to provide it. Dylan thought it was funny. He was a fantastic Papa, so loving and caring. My life was amazing. I couldn't wait to put another baby in Dylan, but he told me I had to wait, much to my disappointment.

We were celebrating Jason's two-week birthday when I heard a car tyers squeal on the path outside as it came to a sudden stop in front of the main house. I looked out the window to see a woman who looked like she was on a mission.

Jasper came out of the main house; his face was as dark as thunder.

"Fucking take some fucking responsibility," the woman screamed. I stormed outside and straight towards where the woman was standing still screaming at Jasper, who of course couldn't hear a word she was fucking saying.

"What the fuck?" I roared, shutting the woman down immediately. No one yelled at my brother. No one spoke to him like he was some piece of shit.

"Make him fucking understand," she screamed again. From her scent I could tell she was a shifter.

"He can't understand because he can't hear you. He is deaf, you dipshit, it doesn't matter how loud you scream he still won't be able to hear you. Do not come into this place, a place of peace and sanctuary for others and start screaming," I growled back, making sure to keep my voice low.

I was all too conscious of the omegas and children that lived in the compound that would have been terrified of this woman's yelling. We tried so hard to keep it a place of peace. Too much shit had gone on in the omegas lives already.

The woman deflated in front of me and scrubbed her hands up over her head, threading them through her hair and tugging on knots. I took all of her in, she looked like she hadn't slept in weeks. Her eyes were red, I couldn't tell from crying or from drugs. She looked wild.

"If you are calm, tell me who you are?" I said as I signed for Jasper's benefit.

"My name is Tara. I'm the mother of Jasper's daughter, Daffodil."

My eyes widened and I turned to face Jasper who was watching me with a look on his face that was the closest I could see to shame. His cheeks were pink, and he barely was able to meet my eyes.

Is it true? I signed. *You have a daughter?*

Jasper didn't sign back but nodded his head. I turned back to Tara and looked at her. "How did we not know about this?"

Tara snorted. "I was Jasper's dirty little secret. He liked to come and fuck me, but the minute I got pregnant he disappeared."

"How old is Daffodil?" I questioned.

"Six. It has taken us this long to find him. Every time I came here and asked, someone at the guard house told me that Jasper wasn't here. It took me five years just to find this compound."

"Jesus," I whispered with a shake of my head. "Are you mates?"

Tara snorted again and shook her head. "No. I was just easy pussy it seems."

I sighed and nodded. I knew that Jasper was a man whore, there was no shock there. But to know that he'd managed to keep this a secret for six years.

"So, what do you want? Money? What?"

Tara shook her head. "I can't do it anymore. Daffodil, she has problems. I can't. It's just too hard."

"Where is she?" I asked.

Tara turned and pointed at the car. I glanced into the back seat window to see a little girl with blonde curls and big blue eyes staring back out at me. The minute I saw her I knew. Daffodil had down syndrome.

I went to the car and opened the door, crouching down at the side, I smiled up at my niece. "Hello Daffodil, my name is Jai. I'm your uncle."

Daffodil didn't speak but reached out a hand to me and stroked it down the side of my face.

"She can't talk," Tara said quietly behind me.

I nodded my head. "Has she seen specialists? Doctors?"

Tara sighed. "She has a pediatrician who diagnosed her with down syndrome. He wanted to send her to occupational therapists and all sorts of doctors, but I couldn't afford any of that."

I nodded again. Freya's mates, Caden and Creed were occupational therapists, I knew that we could get her help.

"Daffodil would you like to come in and meet some other kids?" I asked gently.

Daffodil's eyes lit up and she nodded her head before reaching out to me. Unbuckling her from her seat belt I lifted the little girl into my arms. When I looked up at the main house, I saw Iver coming down the stairs. I smiled, knowing that the creator had told him to come bridge the gap between Daffodil and the children.

"This is Iver, your cousin," I said as I placed Daffodil on the ground beside Iver.

Iver reached out his hand and took Daffodil's in his. The look of adoration that took over Daffodil's face was immense. It was as if she instantly knew who her cousin was. Like the creator had prepared her. I watched Iver speak quietly to her, and she responded to him by nodding her head. Iver helped Daffodil to manage the stairs of the main house before taking her inside.

I turned back to Tara who was watching the children with tears in her eyes. "Do you want to come in and talk about what you want?" I asked.

Tara shook her head. "I've got all her clothes in the boot of the car. Take her, give her the life that she deserves."

I sighed and nodded my head before going to the back of the car and pulling out three duffle bags filled with clothes. Tara didn't say anything before she climbed into the car and brought the engine to life. Without even so much as a backward glance she took off down the road and left.

I turned to Jai who was watching her. Tears trekked down over his face. I dropped the bags at my feet and pulled my brother into my arms. Sobs wracked his body as he cried. He'd held this secret for six years. I couldn't imagine what that had been like. But the creator had brought Daffodil into his life, and I would do all I could to make sure that little girl got the life she deserved.

The end.

Don't miss out!

Visit the website below and you can sign up to receive emails whenever S L Davies publishes a new book. There's no charge and no obligation.

https://books2read.com/r/B-A-NZRR-IJEBC

BOOKS 2 READ

Connecting independent readers to independent writers.

Also by S L Davies

Breeding Facility
Memphis
Bacchus
Coltrane
Pax
Raiden
Nash

Devil's Advocates
Lynx
Israel
Jai
Jasper
Arley
Zion
Oakland

KINK
Freya
Tanquil

Obsidian Mechanics
Donte

Onyx Rebels
Onyx Rebels Prologue
Hawke

Rigby Brothers
Asher

Schiavu
Schiavu

Standalone
Sisters Revenge
Killer Love
Soldiers At War
Second Chances
Bunny
Caged

Watch for more at https://www.amazon.com/~/e/B0832T8F7Z.

About the Author

S L Davies is an Australian Author living in Country, Victoria. She is inspired by the world around her.

Read more at https://www.amazon.com/~/e/B0832T8F7Z.